'Good, good, good!' *Sidney, age 9¼*

'Lots of excellent detail and good description . . . Really good characters.' *Cerian, age 9*

'An exciting, imaginative adventure!' *Sarah, age 9½*

'. . . six rumbustious adventures, it enjoys blytonesque jollities and gorgeous grotesques drawn by Ted Dewan.' *Amanda Craig, The Times*

'The Thomas Trew stories are always evocative and exciting.' *Write Away*

THOMAS TREW
AND THE KLINT-KING'S GOLD

SOPHIE MASSON

Illustrated by Ted Dewan

Hodder
Children's
Books

A division of Hachette Children's Books

For the real Thomas Trew, and his family,
Linda, Dave and Alice,
with very best wishes

Dear Reader,

Do you wish you could leave the ordinary world and go into an extraordinary world, one full of fun and magic and adventure – and danger? You do? Well, so does Thomas Trew and one grey London afternoon, his wish comes true.

Two amazing people come calling – a dwarf called Adverse Camber and a bright little lady named Angelica Eyebright. They tell Thomas he's a Rymer and that he has a destiny in their world, the world of the Hidden People. And they ask him to come and live in their village, Owlchurch, which lies deep in the Hidden World.

It's a world of magic – what the Hidden People call 'pishogue'. It's a world of extraordinary places and people – the Ariels, who live in the sky; the Seafolk, who live in the ocean; the Montaynars, who live in the rocks and mountains; the Uncouthers, who live deep underground; and the Middlers, who live on the surface of the earth. Not everyone in the Hidden World is pleasant or friendly, and some of them, like the Uncouthers, are very nasty indeed . . .

All kinds of adventures are waiting for Thomas in the Hidden World. And this is just one of them. Look out for the others, too!

ONE

The wizard jamming Thomas up against the tent-wall suddenly gave a loud snore. It was no wonder he was asleep, thought Thomas. Brock Blackbeard's speech was deadly boring, and nearly everyone else at the Magicians' and Enchanters' Convention was nodding off.

Brock Blackbeard was a dwarf, of the Montaynard people, who lived in the rocks and mountains of the Hidden World. Splendidly dressed in furs and velvets and jewels, he was also the Ambassador of the wealthy Klint-King, Reidmar Redbeard. Reidmar had become King only recently, replacing his cousin Magnus Madbeard. Magnus had been a bad King. Some people said he planned to make a deal with the Uncouthers. In any case, he was rather unfriendly to the rest of the Hidden World, unlike the new King. That was why Brock was here, making dull speeches. The Klint-King had donated the magnificent main prizes for the Convention's star attraction, the Trick Tournament, when human magicians pitted their wits and skills against each other – and people from the Hidden World.

There had never been anything like those prizes. They were kept under lock and key in a glass box in the Institute of Illusion in Aspire, and mean-looking trolls guarded them day and night. Made of three different kinds of gold and precious stones, and very valuable, they were miniature replicas of three ancient Klint treasures: the sword of Sindrini, the dagger of Daini and the necklace of Nissa. Nobody outside the Klint-Kingdom had ever seen the originals, which were guarded by a fierce, immortal dragon deep in the deepest parts of the royal palace.

The wizard gave a big snuffling snore and woke himself up. He shook his head dazedly and scrubbed at his spiky grey hair. He took off his glasses and rubbed at his mild green eyes. 'Er . . . oo . . . omph,' he snorted, and sitting up straighter in his chair, twitched his green and gold robes neatly around him. He smiled shyly at Thomas. 'A bit hot, eh, what?'

Thomas smiled back, and got up. Now the wizard was awake, he could at last squeeze past him.

'Er . . . excuse me,' he began. 'Could I please . . . ?'

The wizard didn't hear him. He was staring at something near the stage. In a rather startled sort of way, he said, 'That's odd, I could have sworn . . .' But whatever he was about to say, Thomas didn't find out. For at that very moment, Brock Blackbeard finished his speech.

A storm of clapping broke out. Everyone jumped to their feet and cheered, including the wizard. Brock Blackbeard beamed. He bowed deeply, the rings on his fingers flashing with a thousand fires. Imagine, he must think people loved his speech, thought Thomas, grinning to himself, as he made his escape at last.

He found Pinch and Patch down near the river, as usual. They were racing leaf-boats on the water. Not the usual kind, though. They'd turned the leaves into little golden replicas of ancient Klint longships, complete with oars, billowing sails and dragon's heads on the prows.

Forgetting all about being bored, Thomas flung himself down on the grass and watched the two little ships sail lightly across the water.

'Wow, they're fantastic!'

'We've just thought them up,' said Patch, pleased. 'From a picture in an old book.' The Klints did not use ships like that any more. Brock and his entourage had come in a sleek white cruiser that had glided silently down the Riddle from the sea.

'Sssh, we've got to concentrate, or they

wobble,' scolded Pinch. It was true. The little ships started shaking, collapsing in on themselves. Thomas saw that they were, in fact, still only leaves. Then, with a tiny 'pop!' they swelled back into ship-shape again. Thomas held his breath.

'I wish I could do glamouring,' he said, wistfully.

'You can't,' said Pinch, keeping his eyes fixed on his ship, which was edging ahead of Patch's. 'We've only just been allowed to try this out ourselves. And I don't think we're supposed to teach you.'

'Thomas is a Rymer,' said Patch.

'So what?'

'So it might be different for him. Hey!' Patch had taken her eyes off her ship and Pinch had chosen that moment to race past her. He sent his ship flying to the opposite bank. It rocked a little, the golden prow flashing in the sun.

'I won! I won!' he yelled happily.

'Oh, do be quiet.' Patch's longship was still

some distance behind. She waved at it crossly. Instantly, it turned back into a leaf.

'Bad loser,' said Pinch, grinning. He waved a hand at his own ship, which rose in the air, whirled around once, and disappeared with a bright pop like a bubble. A rather damp and floppy leaf fluttered back down to the water.

Patch shrugged. 'Show-off,' she said frostily.

Pinch ignored her. 'Hey, Thomas, how did Blackbeard's speech go?'

Thomas made a face. 'Bad as you said it would be. Worse, even.'

'Told you it wasn't worth going to, even if the Klints haven't been here for ages,' said Pinch happily. 'Montaynards love going on and on. Did he recite a poem?'

'He did,' groaned Thomas. 'A really long one that I couldn't understand. And he told heaps of boring stories. He nearly drove me mad.'

'Poor you,' said Pinch. 'But we did warn you.' He scrambled to his feet. 'Let's go and get some food. I'm starving.'

TWO

The Magicians' and Enchanters' Convention, one of the biggest gatherings in the Hidden World, was usually run by Aspire, the village across the river from Owlchurch. But this year, both of them had combined to run it, and so the Convention was very big and very busy. Dozens and dozens of tents and marquees and little stalls spread out over the sunny meadows on both sides of the River Riddle.

Thousands and thousands of people had come from both the Hidden and Obvious Worlds, for this was one of the few times human witches, magicians, enchanters and wizards were allowed into the Hidden World to mingle with its inhabitants.

Thomas and his friends headed for the huge food tent, which sold goodies from all over the Hidden World. There were Ariel cloud-cakes and sky-toffee, the seaweed crepes and lobster pies of the Seafolk, the hearty stews and cheeses of the Montaynards, a variety of roasts and puddings made in the Middler style, and even Uncouther breads and strange, sticky black sweets. For at Convention time, even the Uncouthers were allowed to send a few traders up from the Land of Nightmare into the lands above. There were special rules. They couldn't sell really nasty spells. And they couldn't bring any poisonous food. The rules were kept. The Uncouther traders didn't want to be banned from the Convention.

Thomas was tossing up between roast lamb and fried chicken when someone tapped him on the shoulder. It was the wizard.

'Hello again, lad,' he said, beaming. 'Any idea where I might find the Register secretary?'

The Register of Approved Witches and Enchanters was very important. If you weren't on the Register, you weren't allowed into the Convention, or the Hidden World. And even if you were on it, you could be struck off, for example if you stole secrets, attempted to trade in evil magic or brought in uninvited guests.

'The secretary is Lily Lafay, sir,' Thomas said. 'You can find her at my father's place, the Apple Tree Café in Owlchurch.'

Lily Lafay was a human witch who had broken a few laws herself, earlier. But she was quite different these days.

The wizard peered at Thomas. 'My word! So you're Gareth Trew's son! Then you must be Thomas, the Rymer.'

Thomas nodded shyly.

The wizard smiled broadly. 'I've heard a good deal about you. My name's Mercurio, by the way – Professor Augustus Mercurio. Perhaps you've heard of me?'

Thomas stammered, 'Er . . . I . . . I'm not sure . . . perhaps . . .'

The wizard wasn't at all put out. 'Never mind. This your first Convention, Thomas?'

Thomas nodded.

'It's my fifteenth,' said Professor Mercurio proudly. 'But this is the biggest and best one I've ever been to. I guess they've all come for the Tournament prizes. Hope to win one myself. Well, Thomas Trew, thank you for the information. I'll be off and find Miss Lily Lafay.'

And with a cheery wave, he was off.

Pinch arrived at Thomas's elbow, carrying a plateful of brightly coloured cakes. 'Who was that?'

'Professor Mercurio,' said Thomas. 'Have you heard of him?' he added.

'Nah. There's heaps of them here,' said Pinch, popping a cake into his mouth. 'Wouldn't have a clue who they all are. Hey – what did *you* get?' he went on, as Patch came up to them.

'Seaweed crepe and frog-spawn jelly,' said

Patch. 'You should try it, Thomas – it's really nice.'

Thomas made a face. 'Think I'll stick to chicken,' he said.

'Chicken yourself,' said Patch, grinning.

They were so busy talking and eating that they did not notice that someone had been watching them for quite some time. And they did not notice the watcher slipping out of the tent to trail Professor Mercurio as he hurried across the bridge.

Thomas and the twins spent a lovely afternoon looking around the traders' tents. They were packed with magicians buying things to take home – everything from books and pictures to talismans and minor spells in liquid or gas form.

The most popular belonged to a very rich Seafolk trader, Madame de Neptunien. Its walls billowed whitely like a sail, but the inside was filled with a strange, lovely green-gold light. In this floated all kinds of sea-creatures, swimming past in the gauzy light. A miniature seahorse sailed close by Thomas's ear, and he held out a hand to it, but touched nothing at all.

'It's a trick of the light,' said Patch, shrugging at his surprise. 'They do really good things with light, the Seafolk. They add a little distilled sunlight to a little seawater, and then stir a special powder called seamoon dust into it. Then they put—'

'Ssh!' said Pinch, pointing. 'She's about to do it right now!'

Madame de Neptunien was a tall thin woman with long green hair, a dead-white face and four waving arms emerging from the short sleeves of her pale-blue robes. She had those four hands full! In one hand she held up a long-necked beaker filled with a bubbling, clear liquid. In another she held up a thin crystal stick. In her third hand she had a little amber and shark-leather bellows, and in the fourth one a tiny little amber box. 'Ladies and gentlemen,' she called, in a high, thin voice, 'I am about to show

14

you our new line in illusions – one which we're very proud of.'

Everyone was quiet as she gently opened the box, took a pinch of something from it – something that glittered and shone silver like grains of fool's gold – and dropped it into the beaker. She stirred it quickly with the crystal stick. At once, the mixture boiled and hissed, and a thin stream of silver light shot up from it.

In hushed silence, the Seafolk trader put the box away in her clothes. She put the beaker down on a table, grasped the handle of the bellows with two hands, and began to blow, very gently, into the beaker.

'Ladies and gentlemen,' she said, 'the air in this bellows is a mixture of south and east winds, with a tiny dash of west. The mixture was carefully created by one of my top people in our city, Oceanopolis. It contains just the right balance of breezes to make sure that the illusion created is a happy one.' Then she blew, softly at first, then stronger, and as she did so,

Thomas could smell the smell of the sea, sharp and briny. Sharper and stronger it grew, and suddenly Thomas could hear the sound of the sea, too – the thump of surf. Now he could see it – a long line of hump-backed green and white breakers. And now! He rubbed his eyes. The breakers had turned into white-pawed big green cats, pouncing and grabbing at the shore, as if they wanted to play. Now they were a line of white and green horses, galloping as hard as they could; and now unrolling silk and lace spilling out fast from great crystal chests.

Madame de Neptunien blew. The waves turned into a rolling green and blue and white floor, and on this floor, couples were dancing – women with long, flying silver and green hair, men in scaly-silver armour. Behind them was a stage, floating in midair, and a strange musical band: a dolphin playing guitar, a big fish playing the trumpet, an octopus on drums, a mermaid singing. Thomas could hear her voice soaring above the instruments. It was like

nothing he'd ever heard before, like hearing the sea speak, or the wind talk. He felt prickles running up and down his spine, and his heart thumped madly.

Madame de Neptunien put down her bellows. At once, the picture she had created gathered itself up, rolled up into a kind of scroll, and dropped straight into the beaker. She stoppered it with a glass cork. She said, 'And there you are, ladies and gentlemen. That is our latest. It is for sale only to Grade I and Grade IA Magicians, and then only for temporary contracts. We're taking orders now.'

There was a rush towards her, almost knocking Thomas and the twins over. They fought their way out of the crowd and went outside.

'Wow,' said Thomas. 'Wow. I wish I could own some of that stuff.'

Patch said, 'You're not a Grade I Magician. Besides, you know, what looks good in Madame's hands might not look as good in anyone else's.'

'Those people who buy it might find it looks different in the Obvious World,' said Pinch.

'You mean it's a trick?'

'Not exactly,' said Patch. 'When you take something like that from our world into yours, it's never quite the same. But it's still pretty good.'

'It's like a copy, you see,' said Pinch. 'It's like those replicas of the Klint treasures. They're lovely – but not as beautiful as the real thing.'

'How do you know that?' said Thomas. 'You've never been to the Klint-Kingdom, have you?'

'No,' said Pinch, 'but I've heard a bit about it. Hey – look, talking of them, here comes Old Windbeard, better make ourselves scarce.'

Brock Blackbeard, talking rather loudly and waving his hands around, came across the meadow towards Madame de Neptunien's tent. The elegant Mayors of Aspire, Mr Tamblin and the Lady Pandora, were by his side, looking rather bored. As Thomas and the twins headed for the Dream Tent, Thomas caught Mr Tamblin's eye. Mr Tamblin smiled a rather chilly smile. Thomas nodded awkwardly back. Despite the fact they had helped out a couple of times when things were a bit tight, Thomas still wasn't sure what he really thought of the haughty Aspirants. Sometimes he liked them, other times he couldn't stand them. The thing was, you never quite knew where you were with them.

THREE

The Dream Tent wasn't like the other kinds of tents. You weren't shown how to make dreams. Only Hidden Worlders could make dreams. Humans were forbidden to do so. It was a kind of weird personal cinema. You went in, sat down, said, 'Begin,' and at once a kind of silver hood, or mini-tent, would come down on to your head. It wasn't suffocating at all, more like being enclosed in a kind of airy opaque bubble. Then suddenly, on the silver cloth, things would start moving – shadows at first, then coming more into focus. A strange film would begin to play, a film made for you alone, a film that in a way you helped to create yourself, because it came from pictures in your head.

Patch had explained it to Thomas, but he still had not quite understood, until he sat down and the dream-hood came down around his face. At once he felt a sharp sting in his eyes. A beam of light seemed to shoot out from them, straight on to the cloth in front of him. And suddenly there was a deep black shadow, rather like the kind of shadow you can make with your hands against a wall. It was the shadow of a gigantic man, standing near the shadow of a great tree. It was looking around, its head swinging this way and that, and Thomas suddenly found himself shrinking back. There was something very sinister about the figure, that made the hair on his arms stand up, coldly, like needles.

Then suddenly, the shadow moved. Swiftly, it ducked behind the shadow-tree and almost disappeared into the blackness. Thomas froze. Another shadow had appeared on the opposite side of the silver screen. It was smaller than the first one, dressed in flowing robes. It, too, appeared to be looking for something. Thomas saw it stop, hesitate. An arm came out of the shadow's sleeve; it looked down at it, as if consulting a watch. It raised a hand to its head and scuffed at its hair. Thomas felt as though he could almost smell the figure's uncertainty. It turned its head, and Thomas briefly saw the shape of spectacles. Then the shadow began to amble towards the tree. Thomas wanted to shout a warning, but he couldn't. His throat seemed frozen solid. Closer and closer the figure went, closer to the tree and the giant hiding behind it, and all at once Thomas knew that something terrible was about to happen. He panicked. Clawing at the hood around his face, he yelled, 'No! No! Stop it! Stop it!'

The shadows vanished. The hood lifted up. Thomas found himself staring at his friends' astonished faces.

'What happened?' said Pinch.

Thomas felt a little sick. His heart was racing. 'I saw – well – I'm not really sure . . .' He felt annoyed with himself now. He should have seen it to the end. After all, they were only shadows, not real people.

Pinch hopped up and down impatiently. 'Oh, come on, Thomas! Tell us! Just tell us what you saw!'

Thomas told them. When he finished, Patch said, frowning, 'That's strange. It's meant to come into focus, not stay as a shadow. You didn't see anyone's face at all?'

'No. That man, walking along, though – he had a long robe and I think I saw the outline of whiskers and a long nose and specs and . . . oh!'

'What?' said Pinch and Patch together.

'I'm almost sure it was that Professor Mercurio! Oh, blast it, I wish I'd kept looking. But I got scared . . .'

Pinch said, 'I think we'd better go and tell someone.'

'Tell someone what?' The sharp voice made them all jump. Mr Tamblin, with Brock Blackbeard still in tow, stood behind them.

Thomas was startled into speech. 'Er . . . something rather nasty that I saw in the dream-hood . . .'

The Aspirant raised an eyebrow. 'It does happen sometimes,' he remarked. 'It depends on the—'

'Pictures in your head, I know,' said Thomas impatiently. 'But is it possible for someone else's pictures to get into your head?'

Everyone stared at him, including the Montaynard Ambassador. Mr Tamblin said slowly, 'It's possible, yes. But only if that someone is in danger, and only if somehow they've got a bond with you.' He added, 'It's called second sight in the Obvious World.'

'I've never experienced anything like that,' said Thomas.

'It can strike suddenly, if the conditions are right,' said Mr Tamblin. 'As they are, in this place, and with a Rymer. But you'll have to tell me—'

Brock Blackbeard interrupted him. 'By Thoran! I'd love to hear all about it, too! I have never come across a case like this before, though I have read about it. In the annals of the Klint-Kingdom – a very large mass of weighty volumes, I can assure you all – there are a few cases noted when mind-projection caused a good deal of very difficult events, and I believe that if this has happened here today then it will have to be written about exhaustively and at length by someone fully cognizant of the impact of the information.' He beamed. 'Would you not agree with this analysis of the situation, Mr Tamblin?'

A desperate expression had come over the Aspirant's face, but he nodded, rather bleakly. 'You don't mind, do you, Thomas?'

Thomas shook his head. He explained, as quickly as he could, what he'd already told the twins.

'I see,' said Mr Tamblin. He paused, and steepled his fingers. 'It seems like a case of mind-jumbling – that is, perhaps Professor Mercurio was in here earlier and some of his dream was somehow left behind. I don't think it's a serious matter. Still, I'll go and speak to Professor Mercurio, who is one of our most respected guests, and a Grade I Magician.'

'And I'll come with you,' said Brock. 'An intriguing case, this, and well worth noting for my diaries, which I hope to have published as—'

'Quite, quite,' said Mr Tamblin hastily. He saw Pinch's amused expression, and snapped, 'There's nothing to smile about, young Gull. This could be a serious matter.'

'I thought you said it wasn't,' mumbled Pinch, after their departing backs.

Patch glanced at Thomas. 'Are you feeling OK now?'

'A lot better,' said Thomas. 'I'm glad they took over, actually. Tell you what, I've had enough of this place. I don't think I ever want to try out one of those hoods again. Let's go?'

'Yes, let's go and have tea at the Apple Tree,' said Pinch promptly, making his sister snort.

FOUR

But the Apple Tree Café was far too busy for them to get a table. So they went and stood in the long line at Cumulus's bakery. Sadly, everything was sold out before they got to the counter. Pinch moaned and groaned about it all the way back to the riverbank. 'I wish all those blasted Obbo magicians would go home! They eat far too much!'

He grumbled even more when they got to their spot and found it taken over by a very loud party of witches and wizards who showed no sign of budging.

'Let's go home,' said Patch. 'It'll be quiet there.'

'Mother might be there, though,' said Pinch.

'And if she is, I bet she'll find some job for us to do.'

'She won't be there,' said Patch airily. 'She'll still be out in the woods . . . Maybe even visiting Father?'

The twins' father, the Green Man, was separated from their mother. Once, they'd been forbidden to meet. But these days they saw each other from time to time.

When they got to the twins' cottage, however, Old Gal *was* home. She was cutting and dicing some roots for use in her ointments. She looked up as they came in. 'Ah, Pinch and Patch! There you are! I want you to . . .'

'Oh, Mrs Gull,' said Thomas hastily. 'Pinch and Patch were just helping me investigate something important . . . something that Angelica, er . . .' he gabbled, as everyone stared at him, 'er, that Angelica asked us to do, and we need to collect some evidence . . . and . . . so we came back to . . .'

'Yes, we came back to get a – er, a little jar,'

lied Pinch fluently, getting the idea at once. 'Do you mind, Mother, if we borrow one and go quickly? It's for Angelica. It's important.'

Old Gal looked from him to Thomas. Her eyebrows rose. She folded her arms. 'Really? Do tell me more.'

Thomas gulped. But before he or Pinch could speak, Patch fluted, 'Oh, Mother, it's true. It's about a wizard called Professor Mercurio. He might be in danger!'

Old Gal snorted. 'In danger? I doubt it. Saw him large as life just a couple of minutes ago. Acting oddly, mind you. Very oddly. Rather shifty, in fact.'

'How, Mother?' burst out Pinch.

'Well, I was gathering these roots. I came across him near that elder thicket just inside the woods. He was bent over something – a pile of leaves was all I saw. He looked so flustered at seeing me, he went so pale, that I knew he must be hiding something.'

'What did you do?' said Patch.

'Well, nothing, really. I just said, "Good afternoon, Professor Mercurio," and went on my way.'

'You mean you didn't try and find out what was under those leaves? Oh, Mother!'

'You don't understand. He's hardly the sort of fellow to do anything illegal. He's been visiting for years, and he's completely trusted. I suppose he was practising for the Tricks Tournament and didn't want me to see. Now, then, if you don't want a job, get out,' said Old Gal briskly. 'I'm very busy. You mind you get back here by dark,' she added to her children, 'or you'll be grounded tomorrow, and I mean that. Understand?'

'Oh, yes, Mother,' Pinch and Patch chorused, and the three of them scampered quickly off.

Outside, Thomas said, 'You know what? I think there's something really fishy going on, around that Professor. We should go and find out what he was doing in the woods.'

Pinch shrugged. 'Why? Mother was probably

right. He was just practising.'

But Thomas shook his head. 'I think it's more than that. He looked really startled by something he saw in the tent where Brock was speaking. And later he asked me where he could find Lily Lafay, to ask her about the Register of Approved Witches and Enchanters. Then I saw him in that dream, and now your mother's seen him skulking around in the woods. What is he up to?'

'I don't know,' said Patch, 'but I reckon you're right. We should find out. But I think we should go and speak to Lily first. She might tell us what he wanted to know.'

FIVE

Lily wasn't at the Apple Tree. A rather harassed Gareth said she'd gone over to Aspire. Had she seen Professor Mercurio? Not that he knew of. And no, the Professor hadn't come to the café. If Thomas and the twins were so bored and had so much time on their hands that they could waste it asking a lot of silly questions, maybe he could find some work for them – washing-up, maybe.

They escaped, quickly, and headed for the woods. They soon found the elder thicket, and the pile of leaves too. They were just ordinary leaves – elder and oak and hazel leaves, in different stages – some green, some yellow, some red, some brown, some mere lacy skeletons. Thomas and the twins raked through them, but found nothing more exciting than a couple of bedraggled feathers and some mud.

'Just as I thought,' said Pinch, folding his arms. 'Nothing to see.'

Thomas ignored him. Picking up a lacy leaf, he dropped it into the little jar he had taken from Old Gal's. He put the jar back in his pocket. He said, 'Well, maybe we should think of it another way. Anyone looking at those little ships you glamoured out of those leaves, before, would think they were real ships, not leaves, and—'

'Wrong,' said Pinch. 'Only humans would think that. Hidden People would know them for what they are at once.'

'Sure, sure,' said Thomas impatiently, 'but just listen. What if these leaves were glamoured? I mean, if they were something else that had been glamoured. If you know what I mean,' he finished rather lamely.

'You're making my head spin,' Pinch began,

but Patch sat back on her heels and stared at Thomas. 'I think you're on to something!' She snatched up a couple of leaves from the pile, sniffed at them, touched their edges. She looked at Pinch. Silently, she handed him the leaves. He smelled them in his turn, and crimped the edges with his finger. 'Hmm . . . You could be right . . .' he said slowly.

'You know I am,' said Patch crossly. She turned to a baffled Thomas. 'There's a smell hangs around things that have been glamoured – *you* can't smell it, but we can. It quickly gets fainter and disappears altogether an hour after the things have gone back to their proper shape. But it's unmistakable.'

Thomas exclaimed, 'Then those leaves . . .'

'Have been glamoured, yes. The smell's still quite strong. This was a strong spell. And Professor Mercurio must have done it.'

'You said humans weren't allowed to do glamouring,' said Thomas.

'We didn't say humans weren't allowed. We

said we didn't know if we were supposed to teach *you*,' said Patch.

'Yes, but Lily, she got into trouble when she did it,' argued Thomas.

'Only because she wasn't an approved witch,' explained Pinch. 'She was unregistered, see. She was a kind of gatecrasher into our world. But the Professor is registered. Besides, in the Tournament they're allowed to use a bit of glamouring.'

'But only a bit,' said Patch, 'and I think he must have used a lot on this stuff. It's a much stronger spell than he's meant to use. Thomas is right. There is something weird going on.' She paused. 'You remember that vision you saw in the dream-hood, Thomas? Could it be set here?'

Thomas shrugged. 'I just saw the shadow of a tree. It could have been any tree, any place, really. And you know how shadows look different from the real thing, anyway.'

'Oh dear,' said Patch gloomily. 'We're stuck.'

'No,' said Thomas, brightening. 'Let's go and look for the Professor.'

'And ask him questions about what's going on? But what if he doesn't want to answer us? What if he's up to no good?' said Pinch.

'Well, we won't ask him anything, then. For the moment, we'll just follow him, see what he does, and what happens.'

'If he catches us snooping on him,' said Patch, 'he won't like it. We'll get into trouble. And not just from him. He's a respected wizard!'

'He won't catch us,' said Pinch gleefully. 'Not if we use a bit of thinning at the right moment!'

'Thinning' is becoming invisible. The twins had taught Thomas how to do it. As a human, he couldn't stay 'thinned' for long, because otherwise he'd get a dreadful itch. But he could do it for a little while, and the twins for much longer.

They left the woods and hurried down to the village. If they'd turned their heads and looked back at where they'd come from, they might have seen someone climbing down from his hiding place in the branches of a tree. But they didn't look back, and so they never knew.

SIX

For the next hour, Thomas and the twins searched through Owlchurch. No Professor. They looked through the tents on this side of the river. No Professor. They crossed over the bridge and searched through the tents on the other side. No Professor. They walked into Aspire. No Professor in the streets. They went into the bakery. He wasn't there. They went into Frosty's, the glamorous Aspire café. He wasn't there. They went into Dr Fantasos's Dream Workshop. Or there, either. They went into the Institute of Illusion. And there he was, standing in line with a crowd of other witches and wizards waiting to gawk at the Klint-King's golden prizes. He saw Thomas at once.

'Hello, young Thomas! Coming to see the goodies again, are you?'

Everyone turned around to look. Thomas felt himself blushing. 'Er . . . yes, I suppose so.'

'Come in with me,' boomed the Professor. 'And your friends,' he said kindly, beckoning to the Gull twins, who were trying to slink away. 'Thomas, introduce me to them.'

'Er . . . this is Pinch and Patch Gull,' said Thomas.

'Ah! Old Gal's children! Pleased to meet you!' shouted the Professor happily, as everyone else in the line stared at them.

Thomas wished he'd be quiet. The trolls were glancing over to see what the commotion was. And you definitely did not want to get on their wrong side! They were bigger and heavier than any human bouncer in the Obvious World, and nearly as tall as giants or Ariels. Trolls had always worked as soldiers and security guards for the Montaynards. People were scared of them. They were rough, violent, and their mean little eyes didn't miss much.

The line shuffled forward. Now they were at the display case. Thomas glanced quickly in at the prizes, which he'd already seen the day before. They looked just as beautiful as ever, shining on their velvet cushions.

He started as one of the trolls spoke. 'Like to win these, eh, lad?' he rasped.

'He's a Rymer, not a magician; he doesn't take part in the Tournament,' said the Professor, before Thomas could answer.

The troll nodded. 'Ah,' he said. 'A Rymer.' The little eyes rested thoughtfully first on Thomas and the silent twins, then on the Professor. The Professor took no notice. He peered very closely at the prizes. There was a little frown between his eyebrows.

'*You* would like to win these, then, sir,' offered the troll.

The Professor nodded. 'Of course. What magician would not?' He straightened up. The

little frown was still on his face. He said, 'Have these been taken out of the glass case at all today?'

The troll looked bemused. 'Taken out, sir?'

The Professor pointed at the case. 'I fancy they were in slightly different positions yesterday . . .'

The troll's face hardened. 'No, sir. No one is allowed to open that case except for our master Brock Blackbeard. He has the only key. And he has most certainly not opened it all day.'

'I must have been mistaken,' said the Professor. 'Oh, well, never mind. Well, children,' he boomed, turning to Thomas and the twins, 'what do you think of them, eh?'

Patch said shyly, 'I've never seen anything so nice.'

'Oh, yes,' said Thomas and Pinch hastily, hoping the Professor would move on. People behind them in the line, annoyed by the hold-up, were giving them dirty looks.

'True enough,' said the troll, pleased. 'Those

were made by Montaynard craftsmen, those were. Master-craftsmen, the cleverest in all the worlds.'

'Yes, I think you're right,' said the Professor, rather absently. He peered into the case once more. His finger touched the glass. The troll moved at once.

'I'm sorry, sir, I'm going to have to ask you to step right back,' he said, his face suddenly as hard as stone. Thomas saw his hand move to the dagger in his belt. He held his breath.

'Sorry, sorry,' said the Professor quickly, stepping back. 'Got a bit overexcited.' He beamed at the stony-faced troll. 'Did you think I was going to try and steal them or something?'

'Please move on, sir,' said the troll, ignoring the question. He waved a hand at Thomas and the twins. 'You too, kids. Scat!'

Thomas felt very embarrassed as they scuttled out of the hall, followed by the curious glances of the other people and the suspicious glares of the trolls. But even more than that, he felt puzzled, and not just by the Professor's odd behaviour. It was something else – something he'd glimpsed, for just a tiny instant.

SEVEN

Fortunately, outside in the street, the Professor was hailed by a friend. Thomas whispered to the twins, 'Did you see it?'

'What he did? We all saw it,' groaned Pinch.

'No, I mean his finger.'

They stared. 'His *finger?*' echoed Patch.

'Yes, when he touched the glass . . . I saw – I think – something shining, on the tip of it, just for a moment . . .'

'What?'

'I think – it was like a grain of silver dust – like fool's gold, I thought – well, it just came to me that I'd seen something like it before.'

Pinch and Patch looked at each other. 'Look,

Thomas,' said Pinch carefully, 'we don't know what you're talking about. Silver dust? Fool's gold? What?'

'That powder – you know – that dust-thing they had in that amber box. In Madame de Neptunien's tent,' gabbled Thomas. 'The pinch of stuff she added to the liquid in the beaker. Remember?'

'You mean seamoon dust?' said Patch, her eyes wide. 'It makes glamouring much, much stronger. But you can't buy it on its own. It's secret. You can only buy the mixture.'

'Then he must have stolen some,' whispered Thomas. He was about to say more, but just then the Professor came back.

'The Convention's always great for meeting up with people you haven't seen in donkey's years,' he remarked. 'Now, then – I'm afraid I'm going to have to leave you, my friends. Something's come up.' He shook hands with each of them solemnly. 'Hope I see you around again.'

He strode off, surprisingly quickly. Thomas said, 'We should follow him . . .'

'Did you look?' said Pinch.

'Look at what?'

'His fingers, of course! I reckon you're right, Thomas! I saw a sort of glitter on his index finger. I reckon he did steal some of that seamoon dust! But why? If he gets caught, he'll be disqualified from the Tournament.'

'Maybe he just badly wants to win those prizes,' said Patch. 'He's prepared to break the law to do a really strong—'

Thomas interrupted her. 'You know what I think? He's very, very interested in those prizes, all right. But I think he's planning to *steal* them!'

'What!' said the twins together, staring at him.

'Are you crazy?' added Pinch. 'Steal them? Did you see the size of those trolls?'

'Besides, he's a respected wizard, and all that,' said Patch. 'He wouldn't do it.'

'Only a really good wizard *could* do it,' said Thomas thoughtfully.

Just then, a loudspeaker boomed over the meadows. 'Would all delegates and guests please gather straight away in the main tent for a very important announcement regarding the Tournament.'

'Hey, look,' said Thomas, pointing, 'the Professor's heading up there, with the others. Coming?' And he scampered off, followed by the twins.

The tent was crowded, and Thomas and the twins had to fight to get near the Professor, who was close to the front. Angelica Eyebright, Mr Tamblin and Lady Pandora came in with Brock Blackbeard. They made their way to the stage.

'Thank you all for coming,' said Mr Tamblin. 'There's been a very important change to our programme. The Tournament will be brought forward one day. It will start at dusk tonight, and complete at dawn. Winners will be announced and prizes distributed when the day has completely risen. Now, please put your hands together for Sir Brock Blackbeard. There is something he wishes to say.'

'They've got to compete *in the dark?*' hissed Thomas to Patch, as the crowd clapped.

She nodded. 'It's traditional. Shh.'

Brock Blackbeard stepped forward. 'I'm sorry, my friends, that we have to hurry this along. But I've received an urgent summons from King Reidmar, and must leave for the Kingdom as soon as prizes are awarded. I hope this will not cause too many difficulties for anybody. I am looking forward a good deal to placing our prizes in the hands of what I am sure will be a most deserving recipient.'

People clapped loudly. Brock looked a bit annoyed, as if he'd hoped to keep talking. But Angelica stepped in smoothly. 'Thank you very much, Sir Brock! We are very pleased you are able to stay to award the prizes. I know it will mean a lot to the winners. Now, ladies and gentlemen, let me remind you that there are two main parts to our Tournament. One is *Hide;*

one is *Seek*. In *Hide*, you get a chance to display your talent for creating illusions and tricks to hide real things, using only the skills we have taught you, and only, as you know, a very limited amount of glamouring.'

Pinch nudged Thomas then. 'Hear that?'

'Yes. Shh.'

'In *Seek*,' went on Angelica, 'you get a chance to display your talent for seeing *through our* illusions and tricks and finding the real things behind them. You will pit your skills not only against the other human magic-workers but also against some of us. As you know, there are several prizes for each section, plus the main prize for Tournament Grand Champion. Together with Sir Brock, we have decided to award King Reidmar's gifts to that Grand Champion. The other prizes will, however, be very good, and include some very fine and rare ointments, potions, books, instruments, and a good deal else besides. Now, competitors, please make sure you have given your name and entry number to Miss Lily Lafay and Mr Gareth Trew at the Apple Tree Café. Assemble here at dusk. And good luck to you all!'

The crowd surged out, separating Thomas from his friends. Patch caught up with him outside.

'The Professor went straight away to the food tent,' she said. 'Pinch went after him. Let's go.'

But the Professor did nothing more exciting than order cakes and tea. The tent was crowded, and he didn't notice Thomas and the twins, so they didn't need to 'thin' at all. It was boring and frustrating. But at last the Professor finished his meal and got up. He went out of the tent. Thomas and the twins followed. The Professor looked at his watch, looked at the sky – it was now late afternoon, edging towards evening – nodded to himself, then hurried along to one of the Montaynard tents. Thomas and the twins looked at each other.

'Better thin now,' said Pinch, 'just in case.'

Thomas held his breath as he 'thinned'. It wasn't pleasant, being there, for 'thinning' was a kind of place too, a sort of cold misty space between worlds, through which you could see what was happening, but not altogether clearly, like looking through frosted glass. And already, the itch had started . . .

Inside the Montaynard tent, it was rather dark, but sort of cosy. Light came from glowing little golden creatures rather like fireflies, who flitted about the tent or hung in bunches from the walls, like living lamps. Pinch whispered that they were called 'blazebirds' and were used by the dwarves to power everything from machines to lamps. By the soft light of the blazebirds, and through the frosted screen of 'thinning', Thomas saw the Professor talking to a rather sour-looking dwarf woman. He crept closer.

The dwarf trader was showing the Professor a beautiful display of opals of various colours. Smooth and translucent, they glowed with a thousand fires, as if someone had carefully snipped off bits of all the underground flames of the earth and woven them together under a crystal globe. The Professor picked up two, paid for them, and went out again, still without appearing to notice that he was being followed. He went on to the Seafolk tent, and bought a little bottle of seamoon mixture, and then on to an Ariel stall, where, after much haggling, he bought two thin blue lengths of sky-rope.

'I think he's stocking up for the competition,' whispered Patch, as they trudged rather tiredly in his footsteps. 'I don't think he's doing anything wrong at all. And he bought some of that seamoon mixture. He'd hardly do that if he'd already pinched the dust . . .'

'Maybe not,' said Thomas. He was feeling more than a little dashed by now, and very uncomfortable in 'thinning'. Perhaps he'd imagined the seamoon dust glittering on the Professor's finger? Perhaps he was making too much of things? He was about to suggest they give up, when the Professor halted in front of a dark igloo-shaped Uncouther tent. At the long tunnel entrance, he paused and looked around rather furtively. The twins and Thomas held their breath, glad they were still 'thinned'. Then the Professor sighed, looked at his watch again, and stooping down, he went into the Uncouther tent.

Thomas and the twins looked rather uneasily at each other.

'I suppose it's got to be all right; those Uncouthers can't do anything bad here, they're not allowed,' said Patch.

'Got to be,' echoed her brother.

Thomas said slowly, 'I think we'll have to go in. We have to know what he's doing.'

'We could listen at the walls,' said Pinch hopefully. 'We know a little spell that will make words louder if—'

Patch broke in. 'Trouble is, everyone hears it, not just us!'

'But we can't go thinned in there, you know that,' said Pinch.

Patch explained, 'You see, thinning can turn into a real Nightmare with Uncouthers about. You can get trapped for ever.'

'Well, then,' said Thomas, popping immediately out of 'thinning'. 'We'd just better be careful.'

The Montaynard tent had been dark, but cosy. This was quite different. The darkness here was thick and heavy and almost alive, like a giant formless animal. Trying to master panic, Thomas crept into the entrance tunnel. It seemed to him that the sides and ceiling were closing in on him. He could hear thin, vicious voices hissing unknown words to him in the darkness. He gritted his teeth and tried not to listen. His heart thudded like a drum. Then he felt a gentle touch and heard Patch's voice. 'It's OK, Thomas. Don't worry. We're here with you.'

'Those Uncouthers can't do anything to us here,' came Pinch's voice, trying to sound jaunty, 'or they'll be banned, like, for ever!'

Thomas hoped that really did matter to the Uncouthers.

All at once, the tunnel ended. They emerged into the main part of the tent. It was filled with an odd ice-blue light. Everything was bleached and blurred and ghostly. Thomas made out the Professor, at the centre of a huddle of people – Uncouthers mostly but also two or three rascally-looking Montaynards and a Seafolk man with a dead-white face, bulging eyes and long green hair.

Patch nudged Thomas. 'Peg Powler's there too,' she whispered, pointing. 'She's a Middler but very dangerous. You want to watch out for her; she lives in a forest pool and snatches people down into her waters . . . She even tries her tricks on us . . .'

Thomas saw the creature Patch was referring to – long, thin, with clawed hands and lank stinking hair like pondweed. He took good care not to meet her eye.

Everyone in here seemed far too busy talking to have even noticed them yet. But what was the Professor doing, amongst all these scary sorts? The kind of magician who bought Uncouther products would hardly be the sort you'd really want to know. He hissed into Patch's ear, 'I think we should get out . . . I don't really want them to realize we're here . . .'

'Too late,' said Patch, as one of the Uncouther traders turned around, saw them, and came towards them.

He was a gruesome sight. Grey-skinned, like most Uncouthers, his head was bald and shining like a seal's head. He only had one bright-red eye, in the middle of his forehead. His mouth was far too big, displaying rows of small sharp teeth like a fish. He was dressed in a black suit that looked as though it were made of hundreds of tiny scales.

'Can Grimgrod help you, darling ones?' he said, in a soft, hissing sort of voice. 'What is it your darkest heart desires? Tell Grimgrod, and he will find it for you.'

Thomas took a step back. 'Nothing . . . nothing . . . it's all right . . . we're just . . . er, having a look,' he faltered. The others seemed unable to speak.

'Can Grimgrod show you our range? Here, come with Grimgrod . . .'

The Professor had still not turned around; he was deep in earnest conversation. Thomas said, 'No . . . er, it's all right – thank you – I think we . . .'

'Come,' said the creature, and took Thomas by the sleeve.

Patch spoke then, in a squeaky voice that tried to be calm. 'You leave him alone, he's our friend, and you'll be in trouble if you try to force things on him, we'll report you to Angelica Eyebright.'

'And Mr Tamblin, and Lady Pandora,' said Pinch thinly.

Grimgrod dropped Thomas's sleeve. Its

mouth stretched into its ugly grin. 'Oh, darling ones,' it scolded, 'Grimgrod wasn't forcing, Grimgrod was humbly entreating . . .'

'Thanks all the same,' said Thomas, recovering, 'but I think I've seen some of your products already – in fact, even the factories – and I'm not sure that I—'

'You have seen?' said Grimgrod, and the red eye flashed. 'You have been to the Land of Nightmare? Ah – but you should have said, darling one. You should have said to Grimgrod you were the Rymer!'

'Rymer?' said the Professor, turning around. 'Upon my soul!' he exclaimed, as he saw who was there. 'Whatever are you doing here?'

'We . . . er . . . we were curious,' said Thomas quickly.

'Dear me, dear me,' said the Professor. He broke away from the others and came towards them. 'It's OK, Grimgrod,' he said calmly. 'You can leave them now. I'll take them out.' He shepherded Thomas and the twins towards the entrance. 'Thanks for everything. I'll let you know what happens.'

Thomas shot a glance at Pinch and Patch. The Professor was altogether too familiar with these dangerous people, he thought.

Outside the tent, the Professor took off his glasses, and rubbed wearily at his eyes. Putting his glasses back on, he said, 'Not a good idea to go in on your own, kids.' He looked crossly at the twins. 'You're Old Gal's children. You should know better.'

'It's not their fault. It was my idea to—' began Thomas, but a glance from the twins made him stop.

Fortunately the Professor didn't seem interested. He said, 'Just keep out of there, like good chaps.' He beamed. 'I think I've got everything now. If you don't mind, I'll say toodle-oo and go and prepare my mixtures. The Tournament starts in less than an hour . . .' And he was off, his robes flapping around him.

'Well,' said Pinch, 'that was a fizzer, eh! Great

idea of yours, Thomas.'

'Oh, leave Thomas alone,' said Patch crossly.

But Thomas wasn't listening. A picture – a memory – was stirring at the back of his mind. He must try and think hard what it was. Because he knew it was important.

EIGHT

Dusk fell. In the main tent, the Tournament contestants, with the Professor among them, filed on to the stage, to loud cheers and flag-waving. Brock came on stage and made a mercifully short speech, and the Tournament began. The contestants left the tent, and the crowd streamed after them. The contestants all scattered in different directions, each one trailing a noisy, cheerful crowd.

'What happens now?' said Thomas, as they hurried along in the wake of the crowd following the Professor.

'You get to watch what they do and vote on whether you think it's good or not,' said Pinch.

'Does that decide who wins?'

'No,' said Patch. 'The judges give points for all sorts of reasons.'

'For instance, whether they follow the three Bs,' said Pinch.

'The three Bs?'

'Beauty, brilliance, binding,' said Patch promptly.

'Binding? Oh, I see. You mean whether it actually works to bind the watcher, to make them believe in it?'

Pinch grinned. 'Yes, that's the point of tricks and illusion, they have to work!'

Just then, Lily Lafay caught up to them. 'Hello,' she smiled. She had a very nice smile. 'Enjoying yourselves?'

'Yes,' said Thomas.

'I'm really looking forward to the Professor's trick,' said Lily. 'He's really good, you know. One of the best.'

Thomas said, a bit too quickly, 'Did you— I mean, has the Professor spoken to you?'

'Spoken to me? What do you mean?' Lily's blue eyes were suddenly sharp. 'Come on, spit it out. What's up?'

'Nothing, nothing,' said Pinch hastily. 'It's just that the Professor asked Thomas who was looking after the Register, and he told him it was you.'

'Oh, is that all? Well, he hasn't come to see me yet,' said Lily. 'Maybe he will later.' She didn't sound particularly interested.

Just then, Gareth Trew came up. 'Lily, you're wanted at the main tent, I'm afraid.'

'Oh, no,' sighed Lily. 'More work. Just when I was hoping to see Professor Mercurio in action.'

'I'm sure it won't be for long. And Thomas and the twins will tell us all about it, won't you?' smiled Gareth. Without waiting for an answer, he and Lily set off, arm in arm.

'They're getting very *friendly*, aren't they?' said Pinch, with a sideways grin at Thomas,

Thomas shrugged. 'I suppose so,' he said, trying to sound as if he didn't care. Truth was, he wasn't sure just what he felt about his father's and Lily's growing closeness.

'Good thing she left, anyway,' said Pinch. 'I thought you might tell her too much. And we don't want the grown-ups to take over.'

'Yes. This is *our* mystery,' said Patch.

'There probably *is* no mystery, though,' said Thomas glumly.

'Don't be such a wet blanket! Oh – look! Where's he going?' said Pinch.

The Professor had not crossed the bridge, like most of the others. Reaching the river, he turned and walked rapidly along the bank, away from Aspire. His followers trotted after him.

'I think he might be going to the jetty,' said Patch. 'Oh, well, that'll be more interesting than the woods or the glades.'

The jetty jutted out into one of the deepest and widest parts of the Riddle. Some of the visitors had come by boat, and so there were quite a few boats moored there, including Brock's sleek cruiser. The wizard marched with a firm step down the jetty and stopped at the edge, right near the water. His audience followed.

'Ladies and gentlemen,' said the Professor solemnly, 'today, I will show you an amazing trick – just how something big can be hidden in plain sight. I will make this—'

He was interrupted by a shout from someone running down the path. 'Emergency! Stop!'

It was Adverse Camber. He was red in the face, panting. 'I'm sorry. You'll have to delay your show. Everyone must return to the big tent. Everyone, without exception.'

There was a stunned silence, which the Professor was the first to break. 'My dear fellow, whatever's the matter?'

'Thieves,' cried Adverse. 'Thieves broke into the Institute of Illusion and stole King Reidmar's golden treasures from under the very noses of the guards!'

'*What?*' The cry came from many throats.

'I'm afraid it's true. They broke into the

display case somehow – took the treasures – glamoured up some leaves to take their place – a very strong glamouring – very powerful – so it looked to the trolls as though the treasures were still there. And everyone was busy elsewhere, preparing for the Tournament. The Institute was almost deserted. But then the glamour faded, and so the crime was discovered.'

Thomas and the twins looked at each other, hearts beating fast. 'Adverse—' Thomas began, but the Professor broke in.

'But the trolls . . . it's rather suspicious they noticed nothing . . .'

Adverse shook his head impatiently. 'They were spellbound – caught in a strong spell-net. They knew nothing. They saw nothing. Come on then, all of you. Get back to the tent. I've got to go and fetch all the others.'

'Adverse!' Thomas said again, more loudly, but the dwarf waved an impatient hand at him. 'Later, Thomas, later.' He rushed off, followed by the crowd, except for Thomas and the twins.

Thomas whispered excitedly, 'Did you hear that? *The thieves glamoured some leaves!*'

'Yes, and did you hear what the Professor said?' whispered Patch, her eyes starting nearly out of her head.

'About hiding something big in plain sight? Yes!' said Pinch.

'I think that—' Thomas began. But he never finished his sentence, for at that very moment, something hard came down on the back of his neck, and he fell into a roaring blackness, shot through with whizzing red stars.

NINE

Ow. Ow. *Ow!* His head was hurting like mad. His tongue felt furry in his mouth. His limbs ached. He couldn't see anything. He couldn't even open his eyes. They seemed glued shut. Or maybe he had gone blind?

'Help! Help!' Thomas tried to shout. But his voice was tiny and useless. And it made his throat sting. He felt around him. He was on something hard, smooth and cool. Wood? Stone? He wasn't sure. He felt a bit further. And touched something warm, which jerked. He drew his hand back hurriedly.

'Thomas?' The whisper, more like a soft croak, came out of the darkness.

'Patch?' said Thomas.

'Thomas?' came her voice again. She hadn't heard him. His voice had been too small. He tried again, forcing himself to speak louder, though it hurt his throat. 'Patch, is that you?'

'Yes,' she said. 'I can't see anything, can you?'

'I can't either.'

'Can you move?'

'I can move my hands,' Thomas said. He tried to wriggle his legs, but couldn't. 'My legs seem to be tied up, though.'

'Mine too,' said Patch. 'My arms as well.' She paused, then whispered, 'Pinch, Pinch, are you there?'

A soft groan answered her.

'Pinch, are you all right?'

'No,' came Pinch's voice. 'I feel like I've been run over by a troll regiment. And I can't see a thing.'

'Where are we?' said Thomas. 'What's happened?' Now he was starting to use his voice again, it felt a little better. But his throat still ached.

'No idea, to both questions,' croaked Pinch.

'Ssh. Can you hear that?' said Patch.

'Hear what?' said Pinch.

'Listen . . .'

They listened. After a moment, Thomas said, 'It sounds like a cat, purring softly.'

Pinch cried, 'I can feel it . . . it's underneath us . . . argh . . . Do you think it's a creature . . . a monster . . . do you think we've been tied up and given to a monster . . . ?'

'Don't be silly,' quavered Patch.

They held their breath, and waited. The purring kept going. But it didn't get louder. Or softer. It just purred. Thomas listened carefully. He thought hard. Then, suddenly, he knew.

'I think we're on a boat,' he said. 'It's moving – and it's the engine that's making the purring noise.' He paused. 'Can you remember what happened, before we ended up here?'

'We were on the jetty,' said Pinch promptly,

'about to see the Professor doing a trick and then Adverse came along and said— Oh, no!' he said. 'Do you think he's kidnapped us?'

'Adverse?'

'No, the Professor, silly!'

'Why would he do that?' said Patch. 'Anyway, he doesn't have a boat.'

'We don't know *how* he came, do we?' said Thomas. 'Anyway, even if he doesn't own a boat, he could always steal one. There were plenty to choose from.'

'But someone would see him and stop him,' cried Patch.

'Why would they? Don't you remember, we'd just learned someone had stolen the Klint-King's gold? Everyone would be off rushing back to the village. Nobody would notice what was happening on the jetty.'

'I didn't actually see the Prof going off up the bank with the others, did you?' said Pinch slowly.

'No,' said Patch.

'No,' echoed Thomas. He rubbed at his eyes, scratching away the crusted stuff that was holding them shut. At last he managed to open one eye. But all he saw was darkness. He unstuck the other eye carefully. Still nothing. He peered into the darkness, trying to get used to it so he might begin to see shapes. He said, 'It's really, really dark in here. I suppose we might be in the hold or something.'

'Marvellous,' groaned Pinch. 'How are we going to get out of here?'

'We're tied up and in the dark. We need a spell or something,' said Thomas. 'Don't you know a bit of pishogue that will help us to get out of these bonds?'

'No,' said Patch. 'We don't.'

'Then we've got to get out some other way.'

'But how?'

Thomas tried to think of the adventure stories he'd read in the past. How did heroes escape when they were tied up? Usually, they had a knife, or a sharp stone or . . .

'Hang on!' he said. 'I think I've got an idea.'
He fumbled in his pocket. Would it still be
there? It might well have fallen out when he . . .
Then his fingers closed around it, deep in his
pocket. He said, 'Great! I've got it!'

'Got what?'

'That jar – you know, the one we took up into
the woods.'

There was a small silence. Then Patch
said carefully, 'Er – Thomas – are you
feeling OK?'

'Look – we need something sharp to cut the
rope we're tied up with.'

'But, Thomas,' said Pinch, sounding rather
dismayed, 'a jar isn't—'

'It is when it's broken,' said Thomas, and he
brought the jar down sharply but carefully
against the floor. As he'd hoped, it broke into a
couple of biggish pieces. He picked one up very
cautiously, and even more cautiously reached
for his feet. He fumbled around till he could feel
the bonds. He said, 'They're quite thin, I think

– the cords, I mean. I should be able to slice them easily . . .'

He began to saw away at them, very carefully, because the glass was very sharp and he didn't want to cut himself.

'Are you getting anywhere?' said Patch anxiously, after a little silence.

'I think so . . .' His hand slipped. 'Ow!'

'Careful!' said Pinch, rather late.

'Wait . . . yes . . . I can feel one of them going . . . yes . . . and another . . .'

'Come on, Thomas, come on, come on!' whispered Pinch.

'I'm going as fast as I can. Yes! Here we go. Oh! Ouch! My feet have gone to sleep . . . ouch! Pins and needles . . . wait a sec . . . I've just got to get them moving again . . . Then I'll come over and do yours . . .'

'Oh, hurry, hurry, hurry!' cried Patch.

Thomas wriggled his feet. They felt a lot better. And now his eyes were getting used to the dark, though it was still pretty black in there. He could just make out the small shapes of Pinch and Patch, huddled on the floor, trussed up like chickens.

He picked up the other sliver of glass. Near it was the leaf that had been in the jar. He picked that up too and put it back in his pocket. He crawled over the floor towards the first huddled shape.

Patch.

'You're going to have to stay very still,' he said, 'because the glass is very sharp.'

'Yes,' whispered Patch, sounding a little frightened.

Thomas sawed carefully away at the cords on her wrists. At last, they fell. He gave her one of the slivers of glass. 'You can cut the cords on your feet,' he said. 'I'll go and do Pinch.'

He went over to Pinch. 'Ready?'

'Yes,' said Pinch, holding out his hands. 'That was such a clever idea, Thomas. Really amazing. Better than magic!'

Thomas smiled. 'I hardly think so! But thanks, anyway.'

The cords fell away from Pinch's hands. He said, 'You know, I reckon we need some light in here . . .'

'We do,' said Thomas, 'but—'

'I've had an idea myself,' said Pinch. 'Wait a moment.' Instead of reaching down to his feet to cut the ropes, he held the piece of glass up and began to hum. It started very quiet, then grew in noise till it was like a high-pitched mosquito.

Patch cried out in alarm. 'Be quiet, Pinch, they'll hear you; this is no time to be glamouring!'

'Quiet yourself,' said Pinch. 'It's coming . . . it's coming . . .'

And in his hands, suddenly, there was a tiny lamp, with a golden flame flickering behind glass, and Pinch's gleeful face lit up by it. 'How do you like that, eh?'

'It's fantastic!' said Thomas. 'Was that the bit of glass?'

'Yes. You see, when you glamour stuff, the thing you use has to have some connection with the thing you turn it into. You can't just turn any old thing into any old thing. Like, see, those leaves we turned into boats, that's because leaves can float, like boats. And glass, well, that has something to do with letting in light, see, and also, lamps are made of glass, and so on. Get it?'

'Kind of,' said Thomas, grinning.

'But now I've got to come and cut your cords, because a lamp isn't much use as a knife,' said Patch, hobbling over to her brother.

'Easier to cut stuff though when you can see what you're doing, eh?' crowed Pinch. 'And when you've done it, Patch, turn your bit into a lamp too! Quick, because the glamour won't last that long!'

No sooner said than done. Now the whole place was lit up by the soft glow of the little lamps. It was plain that Thomas had been right. They were in some kind of boat hold, whose smooth wooden floor moved a little under their feet. The hold was empty, except for a couple of chests in one corner, one on top of the other. There was a trapdoor in the ceiling, with steps leading up to it. Thomas went up the steps and tried the trapdoor, but it was locked, of course.

Meanwhile, Pinch and Patch were examining the chests. They managed to open the first one easily enough. It was full of blankets and sheets. They searched through them but there was nothing hidden in between them, apart from dried lavender.

The other chest, underneath, was padlocked shut.

'I bet you the treasures are in there!' said Patch excitedly.

'We'll have to get it open,' said Thomas.

'Yes, but that other chest is heavy,' said Pinch.

'Not if we take all the blankets and sheets out,' said Thomas. 'Then we'll easily be able to lift it off.'

Carefully, they lifted the empty chest off the

second one. They looked at the padlock. Thomas bent down and fiddled with it, trying to work out a way in which they could break it.

'I think we'll have to—' he began, then stopped abruptly. He had heard a sound. A knocking sound, faint but still clear. *And it was coming from inside the locked chest!*

TEN

'S omeone's in there!' cried Thomas. He bent right close to the lid of the chest, and said, 'Hello? Hello?'

For answer, there was a muffled groan.

'We've got to get it open,' said Thomas. He looked hopefully at the twins.

'No, it's no use, we don't know any padlock-breaking spell,' said Pinch.

'What about glamouring something into a crowbar or a picklock or something?'

'There's nothing you could use to do that,' said Patch. 'Blankets and sheets are no use to us at all.'

Thomas looked in the empty chest. There was nothing there except scraps of lavender. He picked up a lavender spear. 'Couldn't you turn it into a picklock? Or a key?'

'No. It has no connection with those things. Anyway, you know, even if you glamoured up a key, you couldn't use it to actually open things. That's not how glamouring works. The chest is a real thing, you see. The lock is a real lock. A glamoured key won't open it.'

'Could you maybe melt it, if you turned the lamp into say a welder's torch?'

Pinch and Patch looked puzzled. Thomas explained. Pinch shook his head. 'No. It's just as Patch says. You can't use a glamour against a real thing, except in very rare cases. We couldn't have glamoured that piece of glass into a knife that would cut the cords, for instance. The only way you could do it is if it already was at the heart of its nature to do that. Do you see?'

'Not really,' said Thomas.

'Well, it's like this . . .' said Pinch. He broke off suddenly. There was a sound from above their heads. The sound of slow, heavy footsteps!

Someone was walking towards the trapdoor! Thomas thought fast.

'Quick, lift the empty chest back on the other one, shove the blankets back behind them, then get back on the floor, pretend we're still tied up and out to it . . .'

It was all done very quickly. As Thomas scrambled to arrange the cords on his feet so it looked like they were still holding him, he noticed the rope was of a beautiful deep blue that glowed a little in the lamplight. It looked familiar. But he didn't have much time to think about it before Pinch turned the lamps back into bits of glass.

The trapdoor creaked open. Daylight flooded in through the opening. Thomas had his eyes half closed, and through the slit he could see a shadowy figure against the light – a big, bulky figure. Though he couldn't see the face – it was in deep shadow – he recognized it at once. He held his breath. But nothing happened. For a moment, the figure was outlined against the light. Then darkness fell again as the trapdoor was slammed shut and locked again.

Thomas waited a moment, then whispered, 'I think it was just checking we were still out to it . . .'

'But what on earth was it?' breathed Patch. The little lamps lit up again as the twins very quietly hummed the glamouring spell.

'It was just like that giant I saw in my dreamhood vision,' said Thomas quietly. 'I'm sure it was the same one . . .'

'You know,' said Patch thoughtfully, 'maybe you were wrong about what that vision meant. Maybe that giant thing was the Professor's accomplice . . .'

'That's another thing,' said Thomas. 'Those cords we were tied up with – I'm almost sure those were the thin blue ropes the Professor bought in the Ariel tent.'

'Then it's certain,' said Pinch. 'He's behind all this. But why – why would he have kidnapped us?'

'Maybe we know something – something we aren't even aware of ourselves – something that really fingers him for something big – something *really* big,' said Thomas.

'The theft of the treasures?'

'Of course. What else could it be? And he was messing about with those leaves in the woods. It's got to be him. He glamoured up the replacements, and stole the real thing.'

'Yes – but how did he get into the display case in the first place?' argued Patch. 'You can't glamour a key to open it. Brock Blackbeard has the key, and it'll be a magic key. And then there's the trolls. You saw what they're like. There's no way a human magician could—'

'But what if the trolls – or at least one of them – is in it with him?'

Pinch whistled softly. 'You mean, that giant you saw was actually a *troll*?'

'Could be.'

'But a giant is much taller than a troll.'

'Not if it's a shadow-giant,' said Thomas. 'You

know, a little while back, I had this idea I was missing something – something important about what I'd seen. Something I half remembered. Now I know what it is. See, shadows look different at different times of the day, don't they? They're not always the same size as the person who's casting the shadow. Sometimes they're all squashed up and small, sometimes they get stretched right out . . . Maybe that was why the shadow looked the way it did. And maybe, too, the Professor has more than one accomplice. Remember those people he was meeting up with, in the Uncouther tent?'

'They did look very suspicious,' agreed Patch. 'He could be the leader of a gang!'

'OK, OK, that may all be true,' said Pinch, 'but the question is, why would he kidnap us? We don't know anything . . . not really. OK, we were suspicious of him. But that's all. We don't really know anything *definite*.'

'He must think we do,' said Thomas. 'And

there must be a reason for that. We must have seen or heard something and not known what it meant, but he thinks we do know.'

'But what?' wailed Patch.

'I've racked my brains,' said Thomas. 'But I've got no idea.'

Just then, the faint knocking began again, reminding them of the other prisoner. Thomas went over to the chest. He spoke clearly through the lid. 'We haven't got anything to unlock the chest. We're going to try and think of something. Can you hang on?'

The muffled groan came again.

'I reckon they're gagged,' said Pinch. 'They won't be able to tell us anything.'

Patch was looking around, examining every bit of the hold. She held her lamp up high, looking at the walls, the other chest, the floor. All at once, she gave an exclamation. 'There's something here – here – come, quickly!'

They rushed over and looked at what she was staring at. It was a little brass ring set in the floor, under one of the sacks. Thomas and Pinch looked at each other, baffled. Patch saw their expression. She made a little exasperated sound. 'Can't you see, it's some kind of opening . . .' She pulled at the ring. It came up, along with a very small circle of floor. Patch lay down and put her eye to it.

'I think it's the engine-room ... there's a bit of light in there, though. There's probably some kind of window or porthole or something...' She straightened up and let first Pinch, then Thomas, have a look.

'Pity it's so small,' said Thomas. 'None of us can squeeze in through there . . .'

'*You* can't,' said Patch. 'But we can.' Before Pinch or Thomas could say a word, she turned into a tiny frog which hopped straight down the opening and disappeared.

Minutes passed. The boys waited rather anxiously. They didn't talk much. The person in the chest was quiet too. After what seemed like a long time, but was in fact quite short, the little frog hurtled back up through the opening. As its feet touched the floor, it turned back into Patch.

'Well?' said Pinch and Thomas together.

Patch looked rather pale. 'We're in trouble,' she said.

'Well, what a brilliant deduction,' smirked Pinch. 'In case you haven't noticed, we—'

'No, I mean real trouble,' said Patch. 'We're nowhere near home. We're not even on the river.'

'What do you mean?' cried Thomas.

'We're at sea. We're in the middle of the ocean. I saw it through the porthole. I even saw a shark swim past . . . and a mermaid.'

'Then we must have been out to it much longer than you'd think,' said Thomas. 'We might have been travelling for ages. The Riddle's quite long, isn't it?'

'Well, yes, but it does depend on what kind of boat you've got . . .'

'This is a big one,' said Patch. 'You should see

the engine. It's huge. It's made of gold, and it's set in a crystal . . . and there's things rather like blazebirds madly working away in there, and—Oh!' she broke off. 'Of course . . .'

'It's Brock Blackbeard's boat!' Pinch finished for her. 'Who else would have a gold engine powered by blazebirds? That Professor sure has a nerve, stealing the Klint boat as well as the Klint prizes!'

'Where's he going with it, though? Why has he headed out to sea?' wondered Thomas.

'There's all kinds of border crossings from the Obvious World into the Hidden World,' said Patch. 'Usually humans cross at their closest frontier. Maybe this is a quick way for him to get there.'

'But can a human magician pilot a Hidden World boat? Or run Hidden World machines of any sort? I mean, you'd think that it wouldn't obey him! I've tried to get Metallicus to start up for me, and he won't. Won't do it for anyone but Adverse or Angelica.'

'That's Metallicus,' grinned Pinch. 'Contrary old thing.'

'Thomas is right, though,' said Patch, frowning. 'A boat like this wouldn't take orders from a human, even if he's a good magician.'

'Then his accomplices have done it for him,' said Pinch impatiently. 'Trolls or Uncouthers or renegade Seafolk or whatever. It doesn't matter. What matters is – what are we going to do?'

'It's obvious, isn't it?' said Thomas. When the other two stared at him, he said, 'They'll have tools down in that engine-room. We just need to get something – a spanner, a hammer, something, to break the padlock, and then we can get into the chest and let that person out and . . .' He saw their expressions. 'OK, OK, so you don't need tools here to fix anything. But what about capturing some of those blazebird things and using them to melt the padlock? And then we can also get them to burn a bigger hole in this floor, then we can all escape through here and—'

'Into the sea?' said Patch. 'It's dangerous out there, and not only for you. The Seafolk realms aren't exactly peaceful, you know. And you never know which one you might be crossing right now.'

'Well, boats often have life-rafts, and—'

'In your world. In our world you just don't go wandering off uninvited into Seafolk territory. It's asking for trouble. We'll have to stay on the boat.'

'But then – who's to know where they're going? What if the Prof is in league with General Legion Morningstar and the Uncouthers? I know his mother forbade him to stir up trouble any more, but I'm sure he could easily ignore that.'

'It could be true,' said Pinch slowly. 'I've heard there's an entrance to the Land of Nightmare through a black whirlpool in the middle of the ocean . . .'

'That does it,' cried Thomas. 'We've got to get out of here. I'll go first, if you like. Rymers are supposed to have safe passage through all the Hidden World, isn't that right?'

'Yes, but—'

'But nothing. I think it's our only chance. I don't want to end up sucked down through a whirlpool into Nightmare! Come on, Patch. Please – will you get some of those blazebirds?'

'Yes, come on, Patch. I'll come with you and help so we can get lots of them,' said Pinch kindly.

Patch sighed. 'OK. But if it doesn't work, don't blame me.'

ELEVEN

The blazebirds proved surprisingly easy to catch. Pinch and Patch simply turned into frogs, hopped down into the engine-room, shot out long, sticky tongues and captured whole bunches of the little glowing creatures. Then the little frogs hopped back up, deposited the blazebirds in Thomas's cupped hands, and turned back into their own shapes. Each then took a few of the blazebirds. Thomas and Patch went to the chest; Pinch began to work at directing the blazebirds' golden fire to the opening in the floor.

Carefully, Thomas and Patch aimed at the lock itself. They must not set fire to the chest! Things seemed to go very slowly. The black metal of the padlock was thick, and the blazebirds' fire not very strong. To make matters worse, it seemed to be getting fainter by the second.

'It's working! It's working!' said Pinch. The wood was beginning to burn; fire was creeping around the edges of the opening.

Patch whispered, 'If the worst comes to the worst, Thomas, we're going to have to leave the other prisoner here, and try and get help . . .'

'We can't do that,' said Thomas. 'You can't leave him or her with thieves and gangsters in league with the General. Anything could happen to them. Besides, it could be anyone. It could even be your mother!'

Patch's eyes widened. She looked suddenly very scared. 'Do you really think . . .'

'I don't know,' said Thomas. 'I just know we can't leave them here by themselves . . . Ah, look, Patch!' The metal of the padlock bolt was beginning to glow. But they didn't have much time to be pleased, for suddenly, all of the blazebirds in Thomas's hand went out. They lay there like little dead twigs.

'They're exhausted,' said Patch anxiously, trying to shield her own handful. She blew gently on them. 'Come on, my beauties. Come on. Come on!'

The blazebirds glowed a little more. The padlock bolt went red, then gold, then white. All at once, a piece melted and slid off. Then another, and another. Very soon, the padlock bolt was completely gone, and the padlock itself fell with a bit of a crash on to the floor, just as the light of the blazebirds in Patch's hand went out.

Everyone froze. Would the crash be heard up above? They waited for what seemed like ages. The trapdoor did not open. No one came. All was quiet.

Very carefully, Patch and Thomas wrestled with the lid of the chest. It was pretty stiff, but at last they managed to open it. They flung it up. And stood open-mouthed, staring, at the person revealed there, tightly bound, gagged, eyes rolling. Pinch, too, was so astonished that he dropped his blazebirds and they immediately flew down the opening, which was now much bigger, and disappeared.

'Grrmph,' said the prisoner pleadingly. 'Hrrmph . . . hrmph . . .'

Thomas was first to move. He knelt down beside the chest and quickly untied the gag. 'Well, bless my soul,' said Professor Mercurio rather weakly. 'I must say I'm pleased to see you, my friends!'

Pinch and Thomas picked up the slivers of glass. The Professor looked at them in alarm. 'Ah, no need for that,' he said. 'Put them away in your pockets, there's good chaps. Now wait a second. They took all the stuff I bought for the Tournament – but I hope they didn't find something else – some nice little Snappers. Bought 'em just yesterday off a Middler stall . . . excellent for this job . . . couldn't get to 'em of course, tied up like this . . . Just rummage deep

in my pockets, Thomas. Yes, yes, that's them!'

The Snappers looked like tiny scissors. They fitted snugly into a beautiful little green thimble shaped like an acorn. They didn't look like they could cut anything stronger than a bit of tissue paper. But as Thomas opened their blades and brought them closer to the cords, suddenly they turned into a pair of snapping jaws with very sharp needle teeth. They bit hungrily into the cords, dissolving them almost at once. In a twinkling, the Professor was free.

He wriggled his toes and his fingers. 'Ah! That's better!'

The children stood watching him, in the greatest astonishment and embarrassment. All those things they'd said about the Professor, when all along the poor man was a prisoner just like them! They all felt pretty stupid.

'Well,' said the Professor, sitting up and beaming rather short-sightedly at them, 'I do feel like a fool. Thought I was so clever, and I was caught like the most naive apprentice.

Serves me right for trying to spring a trap, eh? Got sprung by it myself, seems.' He felt around in the chest. 'Lost m'glasses. Hope I haven't broken 'em. Ah, here they are.' He pulled them out from under him. 'Drat.' One of the branches was broken, and there was a crack across one of the lenses. 'Oh, well, they'll have to do, for the moment.' The Professor balanced the glasses precariously on his nose. He blinked at Thomas and the twins. 'Care to give me a bit of a hand out? I'm a bit wedged in here, I'm afraid.'

They pulled hard, and finally managed to heave him out. He climbed out of the chest and patted down his pockets. 'Hmm, yes, yes. They've taken the Seafolk mixture, and the opals. Pity.' He spied the cords on the floor. 'And those proved all too useful to 'em! Dear dear.' He stood looking around. 'So we're on the boat, eh?'

'Yes, sir,' said Thomas, getting a word in at last. 'It's Brock Black—'

'Oh, I know,' cut in the Professor. 'Any idea where we are? I mean, outside.'

'At sea,' said Thomas.

'Patch saw it through the porthole,' said Pinch, pointing. 'Down there.'

'Dear, dear,' said the Professor. For the first time, he looked puzzled. 'But why . . . I mean . . . why did they take you children? Me, I can understand, they must've realized I'd rumbled them, but you . . .'

'We thought . . .' Thomas began, then broke off. He didn't want to tell the Professor they'd suspected him. But what if he'd heard what they'd said? They'd been speaking pretty softly, but still . . .

'Anyway, doesn't matter, really, right now,' said the Professor, peering through the enlarged opening. 'What does matter is getting out of here. Can't think we'd be in for a jolly time if we wait till we make landfall at these pirates' lair.'

Thomas and the twins looked at each other. Pirates?

'What sorts of pirates? Who are they, sir?' said Thomas slowly.

'Rascals,' said the Professor promptly. 'Crooks. Thieves. Charlatans. We'll best 'em yet, eh, children?'

'But who—' Thomas tried again.

The Professor ignored the question. 'Getting out means going out into the sea, what? Well, we'll have to hope we're going through friendly territory. Maybe they'll help us get to land. Have to try, what?' He beamed at them.

'That's what I think, too,' said Thomas. 'Besides, Pinch thinks we could be heading for a black whirlpool that—'

'Oh, the water-chute straight down to Nightmare.' The Professor shuddered. 'I don't think these rascals are working for the Uncouthers. Still, you never know. Better be safe than sorry, eh? Though Seafolk country may not exactly be everyone's definition of safe. But I've had good dealings with them over the years. It's all in the way you talk to them. Now then, young lady,' he added, nodding to Patch, 'does that porthole open, do you think?'

'I don't know, sir,' said Patch, in a rather scared voice. 'I didn't really look.'

'Well, we'll have to get it open,' said the Professor comfortably. 'Ready, everyone? You go first, young lady.'

Thomas felt rather annoyed. The Professor was taking over too much. Of course, he was not only a high-ranking magician but also a frequent visitor to the Hidden World. He knew much more about it than Thomas, who had only been there a short time. And the twins hadn't travelled much out of Owlchurch – except to Arkadia. But it was still irritating to be bossed around, especially when the Professor wouldn't answer a straight question about who the kidnappers were. But maybe, thought Thomas suddenly, maybe that's because *he doesn't actually know*. He's just talking big. The thought made him feel better. He followed the twins as they slid through the opening into the engine-room. It was harder for the Professor, but at last, after much grunting and puffing, he managed to squeeze his bulk through the narrow opening.

After the dark hold, the engine-room was rather pleasant. The blazebirds whirred and hummed in a friendly sort of way and the gold motor purred contentedly under its crystal case. Light came not only from the little power-insects, but filtered greenly in through the glass porthole. Thomas looked through it and to his amazement saw that they were passing by some kind of miniature village. He could see little houses made of coral and stone, thatched with weed, with tiny windows made of mother-of-pearl. He could see people looking at them from windows and doorways. They were very small, with flowing silver hair and bluish skin, and black eyes, and tails instead of legs – not only fish-tails but seahorse ones too.

The Professor said, 'Pretty, isn't it ... this lot are harmless tribes, unlike some others, but I don't know if they'll be able to help us. We need some fairly big and powerful transport, you see . . . Still, I'll ask.' He went right up close to the glass and started making signs with his hands, very fast and darting. It was almost like he was imitating a fish swimming down into the depths. Despite himself, Thomas was impressed.

One of the little creatures came flashing up towards them. It stared at them with its bright eyes. Its webbed hands waved around in the water in the same kind of movement as the Professor's; its tail flicked busily. The Professor said, 'He's their chieftain. He says there's a selkie school nearby. They might be able to help us. He's going to send a messenger to them . . .' He waved his hands around in that sign language again. The little creature signed back urgently. The Professor said, 'He says the messenger will hurry. He says that we should try and get out as soon as we can, that the boat seems headed towards a notorious outlaw haven from where there is little escape.'

'But what about being in that sea . . .' said Patch, wide-eyed. 'I mean, especially for Thomas . . .'

'He will be safe enough with the selkies,' said the Professor cheerfully. 'We all will, in fact.'

'But, sir,' said Pinch rather shyly, 'I've heard that selkies keep to themselves and don't like strangers much . . .'

'They're not all like that,' said the Professor lightly. 'It's true selkies can be a bit proud and standoffish, but they are good people, and no friends to the wicked. I think we've got a good chance.' He settled down to wait, sitting on the floor under the porthole, his hands folded neatly. Soon, his eyes closed.

Thomas and the twins sat down in their turn. Glancing at the Professor, Thomas tried hard not to laugh. This was just how the magician had looked the first time he saw him, when . . .

There came a crash from above. The sound of

the trapdoor opening, and the heavy tread of feet! At once, Thomas and the twins were up on their own feet. The Professor, his glasses flying off his nose again, woke up in a big hurry. He tried to stumble to his feet, but tripped, and fell heavily on Thomas, knocking him flat.

'Thin, thin, Thomas, you've got to thin!' cried Patch, and in the flicker of an instant, she and Pinch had both vanished. But Thomas had had the breath and thought knocked out of him. Before he could even begin to remember the thinning spell, there came the sound of running, heavy feet just above his head – and in the next instant, a face looked down through the opening.

TWELVE

It was a broad, brutal face, with little yellow eyes. The face of a troll. Thomas backed away behind the motor. Meanwhile, the Professor had got back on to his feet. Groggily, he searched for his glasses. But they'd been smashed. He murmured, 'Dear, dear, dear, a pretty pickle we've found ourselves in . . .'

The troll was trying to squeeze through. But he was too big. Thomas breathed a sigh of relief. But it was too soon. The troll's long and meaty arm, swinging like a crane, came towards him, scattering blazebirds left and right. They lit on the troll's tough skin, but he didn't even flinch. Thomas and the Professor huddled back, back, as far out of the troll's reach as they could.

But the arm swung closer, closer each time.

'Thin! Thin!' came Pinch's whisper, at Thomas's elbow.

'What about the Professor, though?'

'Never mind him. He can look after himself . . .'

'Indeed I can, lad,' said the Professor, trying to sound jaunty. Thomas looked sideways at him. The wizard was sweating heavily.

'I think we should all stick together,' Thomas said firmly. 'We're going to have to try that porthole right now, even before that messenger gets back.'

At that moment, the troll removed its arm from the hole and put its ugly face there instead. It looked straight at Thomas. 'You wait there, Rymer,' it said. 'I get master.'

'Sure, we'll wait,' said Thomas sarcastically. Trolls must not understand sarcasm, though, for the creature gave what was meant to be a friendly smile and disappeared. They heard its heavy tread above their heads again, going back to the steps.

'Now! We've got to do it now!' yelled Thomas.

Pinch and Patch flashed back into view. Everyone raced to the porthole and tried to tug it open. It wouldn't budge. The Professor hammered at it with a big fist, but only bruised his hand. Meanwhile, the scene outside the porthole had changed. They had passed the little village and were in some dark-green, rather murky water where strange shapes could only dimly be seen. It certainly didn't look very friendly out there . . .

'We'll never get it open!' wailed Pinch.

'Listen!' said Patch. They could hear running feet on the deck two floors above.

'It's too late . . .' said the Professor glumly. 'We can't escape!'

But Thomas had a sudden idea. 'We could glamour the blazebirds into dragons or something – that would melt the glass of the porthole!'

'But you remember what I told you about

glamouring things . . .' began Pinch.

'Yes, but you said that it can only work like this if it's at the heart of their nature. That's fire, isn't it? Blazebirds are about fire-power, and so are dragons. You're just increasing their size, not changing their nature.'

Pinch and Patch looked at each other. Then Patch said excitedly, 'I think Thomas might be right! Let's try, anyway!'

'Wait . . . wait. There's tons of seawater out there,' grumbled the Professor, 'and water puts out fire so that it will not . . .'

But nobody was listening to him. Pinch and Patch were humming loudly, very loudly. The room was getting very hot. The blazebirds fired up with a hotter and hotter flame. You could see them beginning to swell; then suddenly, whoosh! They seemed to burst out of their skins, like popcorn in hot oil. In an instant they were several times bigger, about the size of mice. Their hum turned into a high scream, their shining wings were like molten metal,

flame poured out of their throats. They flew aimlessly about, screaming. The smell of burning filled the air. Thomas felt his skin glowing fiercely, and his eyebrows beginning to singe . . .

'Help! Help!' cried the Professor. 'We're going to get burned to a cinder! Everyone, grab each other's hands! I'm going to try something!'

They all grabbed each other's hands. The Professor shouted out something in a language Thomas did not understand. At once, the cloud of little dragons stopped their aimless blundering, grouped together, and flew straight at the porthole. There was a loud pop; a huge sizzle; then the glass disintegrated, and the water came pouring in, immediately putting out the dragons' fire and turning them back into their normal size. But it also swept into the engine-room, pulling Thomas and the others apart, turning them over and over, tumbling them straight out into the dangerous sea outside!

For a little while, Thomas couldn't see or hear or even breathe properly. He fought hard to get above the water, but it was too strong for him. He was drowning . . . He could see eyes watching him in the murky depths, wicked eyes, hungry eyes, waiting, he knew, for him to get so weak that he would just give up . . . Then suddenly, he felt something nudging up under him, something with a smooth back. He heard a laughing voice. 'Come on, human, hold on, hold on tight to Delfinus's head!' The back reared up under him, and he realized it was a dolphin's! It reared up a little more and he saw its friendly eye, its smiling mouth. 'Hoo!' the dolphin whistled. 'Hoo!'

Thomas flung his arms around its shining head.

The dolphin smiled and leaped up through the water. In an instant, it was at the sparkling surface, with a gasping, spluttering Thomas. How glad he was to be up in the air, even if it

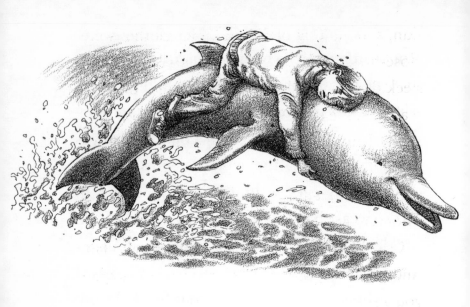

still seemed to be in the middle of the ocean! He hung on to the dolphin, exhausted and relieved. But then he remembered Pinch and Patch and the Professor. 'Oh, no!' he cried. 'My friends! I have to look for my friends!'

Then he heard the laughing voice again, very close to him. 'Your friends are safe, never fear. They're being taken to shore too.'

A girl was swimming along beside him. She was a darting quicksilver creature, with short bright hair under a shiny little cap, and silvery skin, and glinting black eyes. Her clothes were close-fitting, like a gym suit, made of some sleek dark material that made Thomas think of seal-skin. He said, 'Er . . . how do you do?'

She laughed. 'What a funny question! How do I do what?'

'No, I meant . . . oh, never mind,' said Thomas. 'Are you a selkie?'

'Of course! I'm Roanna, of the Protean clan. And that's my friend Delfinus, who's giving you a ride.'

The dolphin turned and looked at Thomas with its cheerful eye. It remarked, 'Hoo! Hoo-mar! Hoo-far!'

'He's saying he's pleased to meet you,' said Roanna.

'And I am too,' said Thomas. 'I'm Thomas. Thomas Trew. I'm a Rymer.'

The girl exclaimed, 'A Rymer! Hear that, Delfinus?'

The dolphin said, 'Hoo! Hoo-kran!'

'Yes, that's what I think too. Amazing!' Roanna

turned back to Thomas. 'Delfinus and I have heard of Rymers. But we've never met one before.' She looked curiously at him. 'What was a Rymer doing in Mirkengrim?'

'Mirkengrim? Oh, I see, that murky place down there . . . Well, I didn't choose to go there, it just happened . . . Look, I can tell you later – but just at the moment – can you tell me where we're going?'

'To the Klint-Kingdom, of course,' she said lightly. 'That's the closest land to here.'

'The Klint-Kingdom? But I thought we were headed towards some outlaw haven,' said Thomas, puzzled. 'That's what that little chieftain said.' He looked around him. The sea was quite empty. 'Where's the boat? Did it sink when we—'

'Yes,' said Roanna. 'Down it went,' she laughed, 'down, down into the depths of Mirkengrim!'

'And the people who were on it . . .'

The selkie shrugged. 'We helped your three

friends, because that's what we were asked to do. The others – they sank or swam, I suppose.' She did not sound at all interested.

'Do you know who they were?'

'No. Should I?'

'No,' said Thomas hastily. 'It's very kind of you to help us,' he added politely.

'It's something interesting to do,' said Roanna. 'Mind you, my grandmother wasn't very happy about it at all.'

'Your grandmother?'

'Hoo!' snorted the dolphin. 'Hoo-zad!'

'Yes, I know! Delfinus thinks Grandmother – who's one of our ruling elders – is old-fashioned,' explained Roanna. 'That's true enough. She doesn't like us to get involved with strangers. She thinks it's dangerous. But she was overruled. And so here we are!'

'I'm really grateful.' said Thomas sincerely. 'And I'm sure all my friends will be . . .'

'Sure, sure,' said the girl. 'But now you have to tell us what happened. I want to know it all, starting from when you came into our world!'

And so as Delfinus moved smoothly and swiftly through the water, Thomas told the girl and the dolphin everything that had happened since he had first come into the Hidden World, right up to the events on board the boat. It was quite a long story, and Roanna's attention was apt to wander. In the middle of a sentence, she would leap up into the air and turn a somersault. Once, she darted down into the water, and emerged with a small silver fish in either hand. She swallowed one whole, and offered the other one to Thomas, who refused, much to Roanna's astonishment. So she gave it to Delfinus instead, who gladly took it.

Thomas had just about finished telling his story when land came into view. He could see a line of tall white cliffs, topped with grass, towering above a curved beach of golden sand.

'Hoo!' said the dolphin. 'Hoo-klint!'

Even Thomas didn't need a translation for that! As they got closer, Thomas could make out a couple of small figures waiting anxiously at the water's edge. Pinch and Patch! But the Professor was nowhere to be seen.

THIRTEEN

When they were still a little way from the beach, Delfinus pushed Thomas into the water, and Roanna helped him to swim into the shallows.

'Hoo! Hoo-ta! Hoo!' said the dolphin, smiling at Thomas.

'He's just saying goodbye and saying he can't come too close or he'll get beached,' the selkie explained.

Thomas waved at the dolphin. 'Goodbye and thank you. I'll never forget you!'

'Hoo! Hoo! Hoo-too!' whistled Delfinus cheerfully.

Roanna didn't stay long, either. She clearly wasn't as interested in the twins as she had been in Thomas, so after brief introductions, she swam back out to where Delfinus was waiting for her. Dolphin and selkie girl leaped into the glittering air, in what was clearly meant to be a farewell salute, then turned tail and swam rapidly out to sea, vanishing in the twinkling of an eye.

Thomas looked after them. 'They were fun. I hope I'll see them again.'

'Hmm,' said Patch a little sharply. 'Maybe you will and maybe you won't.'

'Nasty old sea, anyway,' grumbled Pinch. 'Not half as nice as a river.'

Thomas looked at them, a little surprised. Were the twins jealous? But he said nothing about it. Instead, he said, 'The boat sank, you know.'

'We know,' said Pinch.

'Do you know what's happened to the Professor?'

'No!' snapped Patch.

'*Sorry!* I was just asking.'

A rather prickly pause followed, then Patch laughed and said, 'Sorry, Thomas. We just didn't enjoy the trip. The selkie who took us was whiskery and gruff and kept saying children should be seen and not heard when we asked him questions.'

'And he kept saying that Middlers had no place in the sea and what did we think we were doing hobnobbing with humans anyway,' added Pinch.

'Oh, dear, I'm afraid he must have been a friend of Roanna's grandmother,' grinned Thomas, and then of course he had to explain.

'Just our luck to get the cranky selkie and you get the nice one,' grumbled Pinch.

'And we didn't have any comfy dolphin back to ride on,' sighed Patch. 'We had to turn into frogs and ride on that crabby old creature's knobbly shoulder . . .'

Thomas laughed. 'Oh, well, we're here safely, that's the main thing.' He looked out to sea. 'Still no sign of the Professor, though.'

'Maybe he got here before us,' said Pinch.

'Maybe he's already gone to find the Klints,' said Patch.

'Maybe,' said Thomas thoughtfully. After all, the Professor had been playing a lone hand from the beginning. He hadn't trusted anyone with his suspicions. He had tried to spring a trap and been caught. And he hadn't told Thomas and the twins who he suspected was behind all this. Thomas remembered his annoyance with the bossy old man. 'Yes,' he said decidedly. 'We shouldn't wait for him.'

'I agree,' said Pinch promptly.

'And so do I,' said Patch.

So they set off up the beach towards the path that led up to the cliff-tops. On the way, Pinch pointed out a set of human-sized footprints in the soft sand. 'I bet you those are his.'

The cliff-path was stony and steep and quite long, but at last they were on the top, and could see what lay beyond. It was the strangest, the bleakest, and the rockiest place Thomas had

ever seen. Directly in front of them was a patch of pale, dusty ground, scattered all over with pebbles and boulders, and beyond that stretched a jumble of tall, twisted rock formations pockmarked with holes. It was very still, and quite empty of people, animals, birds, anything at all. Yet there was an odd, uneasy feeling in the air, as if unseen eyes were watching them . . .

Pinch and Patch didn't look too happy either. Pinch said, 'Well, I heard that Klint country was rather ugly, but I didn't know it was as ugly as this . . .'

'But they don't live on the top, you see,' said Patch. 'They live in the cracks of the rocks, and deep inside them.' She pointed at the holes in the rocks. 'I think those are Klint houses. The selkie said that the King's palace is somewhere in the middle of that rocky stuff. But he also said we needn't think we'd get to see him, that there's some big trouble going on and that they wont be pleased to see us.'

'They've probably found out about the robbery,' said Thomas, nervously glancing around. 'They're probably furious.'

'Yes, and Middlers won't be popular,' said Pinch, 'because it was in Middler country that the gold prizes were stolen and the Klints humiliated.'

Thomas exclaimed, 'Hey – what if they *meant that to happen?* I mean, the thieves. What if it was all a set-up, if the point was to stir up trouble between the Klints and the Middlers? The Professor reckoned the thieves didn't have any links with the Uncouthers, but I don't think he really knew.'

'But those prizes are worth heaps,' said Pinch. 'Any thief would want to steal them!'

'Yes, but if they were just ordinary thieves, why didn't they steal the gold before? I mean, when it was on its way to the Convention? They could have hijacked Brock's boat at sea and taken the gold prizes then. Less risky than waiting till they were in Aspire, with lots of people watching. I think that's really fishy. They wanted to make a big stink, to make Owlchurch and Aspire look really stupid and useless for getting taken in by glamour and not protecting the prizes properly.'

'Hang on,' said Patch. 'If the thieves were human magicians, though, they couldn't do it anywhere else than at the Convention. They only have passports for that. They can't just wander into Seafolk territory and . . . Oh!' She broke off.

'Yes,' said Thomas. 'That's right. The Professor went into Seafolk territory, so why can't other magicians?'

'That's different,' said Pinch, but he looked thoughtful.

'Anyway the thieves don't have to be humans,' added Patch. 'They could be anything, really.'

'Uncouthers, I bet,' said Pinch darkly.

'Or maybe outlaws from somewhere else,' said Patch.

'Well, there's only one thing to do,' said

Thomas. 'And that's to go and see the Klint-King and tell him everything.'

'What if he's not friendly? What if he locks us up, or worse?'

'We'll have to risk it,' said Thomas, more bravely than he felt.

'The Professor's probably there already, anyway,' said Pinch.

'So what? We know stuff he doesn't. And besides, we don't know what he's really up to.'

'You don't really still suspect him?' asked Patch.

'I'm not sure. But he hasn't exactly explained everything, has he?'

'He sure hasn't,' growled Pinch. 'OK, then. Let's get going.'

FOURTEEN

Up close, the holes in the rock formations were like yawning black mouths, and the rocks themselves were tumbles of menacing shapes, like wild creatures turned to stone. They smelled odd, too – sharp and metallic. There was not a blade of grass growing on them, nothing moved on them, not an insect, not a lizard, nothing. It was very, very quiet. Far too quiet. The path between the rocks was narrow and steep, and Thomas and the twins had to walk in single file. They didn't speak. But though they tried to walk softly, their feet kept dislodging pebbles, which rolled and tumbled down the path, making what seemed like a terrible row, every time.

I wish we'd waited down on the beach, Thomas thought, as they climbed higher and further into the rocks. This wasn't a good idea. This place doesn't feel friendly at all. But they couldn't turn back now. He had a feeling that if they tried, they would be set upon at once.

Pinch whispered, 'I hope we're going the right way.'

'How would we know?' whispered his sister.

In that moment, Thomas thought he glimpsed a pair of eyes staring at him from one of the holes. A pair of bright black eyes, with yellow pupils, that looked very unfriendly indeed. He tried to get a grip on himself. They were in Montaynard territory, not Uncouther country. The Klints weren't enemies. No, they really weren't. They really, really weren't. Everyone said so. To distract himself, he thought through everything that had happened. He was beginning to piece things together, but he wasn't sure if he was right. Not just yet . . .

He looked behind him, and gave a little cry. Pinch and Patch heard, and turned around. 'What's up?'

'Look,' said Thomas, 'where we've just come from . . . We'll never get out again!'

It was true. The path behind them had disappeared. In its place was a solid wall of rocks. The rocks had come closer together, cutting off the way back!

Patch said in a very small voice, 'Then we've just got to keep going . . .'

'Keep going where?' snapped Pinch. 'Straight into a Klint prison, I reckon!'

'We have to explain to them,' said Thomas. 'It'll be OK. We just have to tell them . . .'

He stopped because, suddenly, the rocks in front of them parted wide, with a grinding sound. Behind them was an enormous, round, rocky hill. Cut into it was a large doorway. The door itself was made of pure gold, inlaid with precious stones. There was a large knocker on it in the shape of a dragon's head. The door was firmly shut, but there were no guards near it.

'I suppose that must be it,' said Patch uncertainly.

'I suppose we should knock,' faltered Pinch.

Thomas didn't feel good about it either. But what else could they do? He walked boldly up to the door and, lifting the knocker, rapped smartly, once. Then he fell back in fright, for the dragon's mouth opened and out of the knocker came a loud, ferocious roar that went on and on and on, echoing and bouncing off the rocks, louder and louder, like endless thunder. As Thomas and the twins huddled together in fright, faces began appearing at the entrances of the holes in the rocks all around them. An instant later, the owners of the faces popped out of the holes, and the children found themselves surrounded by dozens of hard-faced, heavily armed Klint men. For all their dwarfish size, they did not look like people you'd really want to argue with.

A blond-bearded dwarf with cropped hair,

who gripped an enormous sword, stepped forward. Holding the wickedly sharp point of the sword towards Thomas, he barked, 'Who are you who dares wander into Klint country uninvited and knock on the Dragon Door?'

Thomas swallowed, but answered bravely. 'I am Thomas Trew, the Rymer. And these are my friends Pinch and Patch Gull. We come as friends to see the King.'

The dwarf's eyes narrowed. 'The King does not know you.'

'But he will,' said Thomas, drawing himself up to his full height, which wasn't much, but more than the blond dwarf.

'Where are you from?' said the dwarf, unblinking.

'From Owlchurch. From the Magicians' Convention.'

At this, the Klint men began an angry buzz, like hornets, and shook their weapons. The blond dwarf held up a hand for silence. 'A grave insult was offered to our Ambassador in that place. Thieves have taken—'

'We know, we know,' said Thomas, 'and we've come to tell the King what really happened and who really insulted him.' He ignored Pinch and Patch's startled glances. He didn't want to show he wasn't really sure of his ground and really only had a few hunches to go on.

The dwarf looked Thomas up and down. 'You speak recklessly, Rymer,' he said softly. 'And if you do not speak truly you will suffer the consequences.'

'Oh, stop being so stuffy,' said Thomas impatiently. 'Take us to your King and you'll soon see if he listens to what I say or not. What have you got to lose?'

Pinch and Patch had turned quite bright green with fright. It was clear they thought something terrible was about to happen. But the dwarf stared unblinking up into Thomas's eyes for a moment before very suddenly and unexpectedly cracking a beaming smile.

'By Thoran! There speaks a brave and spirited

lad! Very well, I, Snori Sunbeard, chief storyteller to the King, will take you into His Majesty's presence.'

Snori Sunbeard, thought Thomas, trying hard not to giggle. What a name for a storyteller! But fitting enough, if his stories were as boring as Brock's speeches. Aloud, he said, very politely, 'Thank you very much. That's very kind of you.'

Snori walked to the door and rapped on it, once, with the handle of his sword. This time, it gave a cheerful bell-like note; and in the next moment, it glided open, revealing a long hall beyond, warmly lit by dozens of blazebird lamps.

Thomas and the twins followed Snori inside, and were followed in their turn by the other Klint men. As the golden door closed behind them, Thomas had a moment of panic. What would the King say when he told him what he suspected? But it was too late now to change his mind, and too late, as well, to consult with

Pinch and Patch. He'd just have to hope for the best.

Inside, it was very different from the bleak, unfriendly landscape they'd just left. The palace was truly amazing. The long hall, hung with magnificent tapestries worked in gold and silver thread, soon gave way to a series of rooms, each more beautiful and richly furnished than the next. Blazebird lamps filled the rooms with bright light; gold and silver ornaments, set with precious stones of every colour, sparkled everywhere. The furniture was gilded and carved, the carpets of the finest silks in jewel colours – scarlet, azure, jade, purple. Troll servants bustled around, and troll guards stood in every doorway. They seemed quite incurious and didn't even look at the children.

Now Snori led the way into a large waiting-room, hung with dozens of painted portraits of grim-faced Klint lords and ladies. There were labels under each portrait. Thomas could see some of them: 'King Etri Elfbeard the First',

'Queen Freya Fairhair the First', and so on. He smiled to himself. If dwarf men's names always had 'beard' somewhere, it seemed dwarf women always had 'hair'.

Snori waved away the other Klint men, and ushered Thomas and the twins into the room. 'Sit down,' he said, motioning to some chairs. 'I'll go and see if we can get an interview with King Reidmar.'

He left them and went to a door at the far end. He knocked, and went through.

FIFTEEN

Left alone, the twins turned on Thomas at once.

'You said you knew what happened! What do you mean? Why didn't you tell us?'

'Because I'm not sure,' said Thomas. 'Anyway, it's like this. I think maybe we were looking at things the wrong way. I think actually the whole thing's a trick. I think that the prizes we saw in the Institute of Illusion were never the real thing – I mean, I think they were *always* glamoured – and that the real ones never left the Klint-Kingdom at all . . .'

'What?' said Pinch and Patch together, goggling at him.

'I mean, I think this was a Klint plot.'

'Are you crazy?' cried Pinch. 'King Reidmar would never do that. He's a friend of—'

'Not him,' said Thomas. 'Someone else. Someone quite powerful. I can't imagine the trolls would do the bidding of someone unimportant.'

'Brock Blackbeard?' said Patch. 'But he's the loyal Ambassador of King Reidmar!'

'Yes, but had Adverse ever met him before? In person, I mean?'

The twins stared. 'I . . . I don't think so,' said Pinch slowly.

'Did Lady Pandora and Mr Tamblin know him personally? Or Angelica? Or anybody?'

Patch said, 'Well, no. It was the first time he came to our country.'

'I see. Why did the King give such a wonderful prize?'

'They're like that, the Montaynards,' said Pinch impatiently. 'They're flashy, and they love to flaunt their wealth. Anyway, I don't reckon you're right, Thomas. You might be able to glamour something to trick humans, easily – but not Hidden Worlders.'

'Rot! What about what Lily Lafay did?' retorted Thomas.

'OK, OK – but those treasures – if they'd been glamoured leaves – I don't think they could last that long,' argued Pinch.

Patch interrupted. 'That's not important, right now! Thomas, you think someone came *disguised* as Brock Blackbeard?'

'Possibly,' said Thomas.

'But who— Oh!' said Patch, her hand flying to her mouth. 'You know, Reidmar's only been King a little while. The one before him, Magnus Madbeard, was thrown out because he was a bad King. What if it was him, taking revenge or something?'

Thomas glanced around. 'Let's see if we can find him in these portraits, see if he looks like the Brock we saw . . .'

'As if he would,' grumbled Pinch. 'He'd make sure to disguise himself!'

They had a good look around. But there was no Magnus Madbeard to be seen anywhere in the portraits on display. 'Not surprising, really,' said Pinch. 'They'd hardly want to keep a portrait of him.'

At that moment, the door opened, and Snori came back into the room, with a lovely young dwarf woman. She had bright red-gold hair in a plaited coil on her neck, and amber eyes. Her dress was of the same colour as her eyes, and she wore a fur-trimmed cloak over it.

'Good day to you. Snori told me who you are. I am King Reidmar's daughter, Gilda Goldenhair,' said the woman rather haughtily. 'You have something to tell my father, but he is busy with someone and cannot be disturbed. You can tell me.'

'Your Royal Highness,' said Thomas carefully, 'we wonder if . . . if there is a portrait of Magnus Madbeard anywhere.'

Snori gave a little gasp. The Princess had turned very pale, and her eyes flashed. 'How dare you mention that name!' she said, in a low, dangerous voice.

Thomas swallowed. 'Please, Your Royal Highness,' he said humbly, 'it's not what it seems. Please, it's really important.'

The Princess stared at him. She said tightly, 'I believe his portrait was taken down and burned. We do not keep portraits of traitors.'

'Does he . . . does he look like Brock Blackbeard?'

The Princess looked astonished. 'What do you mean?'

'I mean, could he pass as—'

The Princess interrupted. 'He could not. For the simple reason that he's dead. Died last year, on the island where he was in exile. Magnus, I mean,' she added, when they looked bewildered. 'It was most definitely Brock Blackbeard who left our shores, with the prizes.' Sharply, she went on, 'It's no use, I'm afraid. Our Ambassador was insulted in your country. The wizard has already tried to persuade my father that there was something that led back to our country in this dastardly plot, but I'm afraid that only increases the insult done in the first place. We are going to have to look at some measures to show our displeasure, and—'

'Excuse me, Your Royal Highness,' dared Thomas, 'but by the wizard, do you mean Professor Augustus Mercurio?'

'I do,' snapped the Princess.

'Is he with the King now?'

The Princess frowned. 'Yes.'

'Will you please – please take us in too? Perhaps, together, we can convince the King that—'

'You are children,' said the Princess sharply, 'and he is a well-respected wizard, even if he is a human. And you only have a ridiculous theory about a dead traitor taking on our respected Ambassador's identity. You will only annoy my father the King.'

All this time, Snori had not spoken. Now he said hesitantly, 'Your Royal Highness, er . . .

perhaps there is another factor in this which we haven't considered.'

She looked crossly at him. 'Just what, Snori?'

He faltered, 'Er . . . Magnus is dead . . . but he . . . his son . . .'

The Princess stiffened. 'I am sure Ralf Ravenbeard has nothing to do with this. He has never tried to take back the throne. He has never tried to raise an army against my father.' Her voice was getting higher, her face was flushed. Thomas and the twins looked at each other, a little puzzled.

'Nevertheless,' said Snori, 'he lives in exile and he has a reason to hate us.'

'You do not know him as I . . .' began Princess Gilda hotly, then stopped abruptly. She glared at Thomas and the twins. 'This is all a cock and bull story,' she said tightly. 'Brock Blackbeard went to your country, with the gold. That I can guarantee. And despite what that fool of a wizard says, there is no way it could be him. He is utterly trustworthy. He is one of my father's closest allies and could not be involved in such a thing.'

'Your Royal Highness,' said Snori humbly, 'I do believe your father would like to hear what they have to say, in person. I do believe it would be for the best.'

'Oh, for Thoran's sake!' said the Princess angrily. 'Take them if you must!' And she turned on her heel and stalked out, head held high. There was a little silence.

'Sorry,' said Snori quietly. 'Princess Gilda is rather highly-strung. And she was once engaged to Magnus's son, you see . . .' He shrugged. 'I'm afraid she still has a soft spot for him. Sadly, I don't share her view of him. Ralf Ravenbeard is clever, bold and handsome, but he's an arrogant young man who believes himself hard done by. What's more, I suspect he learned some Uncouther tricks – some rather dark magic – off his father. And he cannot bear Brock – because it was Brock who advised King Reidmar to move against Magnus. It had to be done – Magnus was a really bad lot – but Ralf would hardly like it. So it would not surprise me at all if he was involved.'

'What does Ralf look like?' said Thomas.

'Not like Brock, really – Brock's black beard has got quite a lot of silver in it these days, and he has a rather sour face. And he's a man of few words – an unusual thing in our people,' Snori added, grinning.

Thomas and the twins looked at each other.

'The man we saw at the Convention was good-looking and very well-dressed, and he never stopped talk— I mean, he spoke very well,' said Patch hastily.

'Doesn't sound like Brock,' said Snori, shaking his head. 'I think the King will definitely want to hear all this. After all, not only has his gold and his boat been stolen – but where is his Ambassador? And his loyal troll servants? Brock always travels with his own men. They'd never betray him.'

SIXTEEN

The room into which Snori ushered them was not at all what they'd expected. It was very plain, whitewashed, with a simple rug on the floor. Comfortable-looking chairs and a businesslike desk were the only furniture. However, there were two striking things about the room. One was the large oil painting on the wall behind the desk, which showed a fiery-eyed, red-gold dragon standing guard over the three treasures of the Klint-Kingdom: the sword of Sindrini, the dagger of Daini, and the necklace of Nissa. The other striking thing was the man who sat under the painting. He was a dwarf bigger than usual, with a wild mane of hair as red-gold as the dragon's scales, fierce green eyes, and a beard as red as fire. He was dressed magnificently, in black silk and cloth of gold, and there were many flashing rings on his fingers, and a heavy gold and emerald crown on his head. There was a sense of power and strength about him that reminded Thomas of someone. For an instant he couldn't work out who – and then it came to him. The man they'd known as Brock Blackbeard! Though he was of such different colouring, there was a strong likeness about them.

Beside him, in one of the comfortable chairs, sat the Professor. When the children came in behind Snori, he jumped up.

'Goodness me, I'm glad to see you!'

But Thomas didn't feel very friendly towards the Professor, who'd not even waited for them on the beach. He only nodded, as did Pinch and Patch. The Professor had the grace to look a bit sheepish.

'Sorry, chaps, but I knew you were safe and I

couldn't afford to waste any time telling the King that—'

'Silence,' said King Reidmar. He spoke softly, but the Professor subsided at once. 'Why are you bringing them in, Snori?' the King added, frowning a little. 'I thought I'd said that I was busy with the Professor.'

'I think you should listen to what they have to say, Your Majesty,' said Snori, bowing low.

'I've listened to enough wild theories and half-baked notions to last me a lifetime,' said the King, shooting an exasperated glance at the Professor, who winced.

'Your Majesty, my investigations thus far have proved that—'

'They've proved nothing at all,' said the King. 'Only that my gold has been stolen and I know that well enough. Do you know what this man has tried to convince me of?' he went on, turning to Snori. 'He has tried to tell me that it was all Brock's doing – that my own Ambassador, my loyal friend, conceived this dastardly plot to steal my gold and my boat and make a laughing-stock of me throughout the Hidden World. He seems to think that the lure of the gold is enough! Well, Brock is one of the wealthiest men in the kingdom, and he has no need of any more gold. Not to speak of the fact that he is a man of honour and would never – *but never* – be involved in such a wicked thing!'

'But, Sire . . .' murmured the magician, 'you must admit the evidence is very strong. At the speech, when he was waving his hands around, I glimpsed seamoon dust stuck to his fingers. Later, I saw him secretly meeting Uncouthers, including that creep of a Grimgrod, and skulking about in places he shouldn't have been!'

'So did *you*, Professor,' said Thomas sharply. 'All those things, we saw you doing them.'

The King frowned. 'Indeed?'

'No, no, boy, you don't understand,' said the Professor hastily. 'I was only detecting – trying to retrace Brock's movements. I was sure he was up to no good. I knew he was doing a spot of secret glamouring – I caught sight of him doing it in the woods; I even found the pile of leaves he'd used. I tried to get them back into the shape they'd recently been. You know, like hitting redial,' he explained, when Thomas looked blank. 'I had to, er . . . borrow a tiny bit of seamoon dust for that – just some that had drifted on to the floor of the Seafolk tent, I hasten to add. But sadly it didn't work.'

'Why did you want to see Lily?' said Thomas.

'I thought at first maybe Brock was some crooked human magician who'd disguised himself. There was one such crook in particular who was a master of disguise – I wanted to see if he had sneaked into the Register, somehow. But soon I came to realize it couldn't be that. I thought then he might be a troll, in disguise. Not for long,' he added, seeing the King's disbelief. 'And then I had to come to the conclusion it must be the Klint Ambassador in person, doing what he ought not to do.'

'Rubbish,' said the King fiercely.

The magician looked apolegetic. 'I'm sorry, Your Majesty, but who else could it be, really? You see, there's this clincher: no one could have got into that display case except for the man who held the key, and that was Brock himself. Those trolls did as they were told – by Brock, their master.'

This was Thomas's cue. 'I don't think it was Brock, Your Majesty. I think it was someone pretending to be Brock.'

'No, no,' said the Professor fretfully. 'I already told you . . .'

'Not a human magician, and not a troll either,' said Thomas.

'Surely you can't think an Uncouther—' began the Professor.

The King flapped a cross hand at him. 'Do be quiet, Professor. Let Thomas finish.'

'I think this man was from . . .' Thomas swallowed, then continued, 'your own people, King Reidmar.'

'What!' shouted the King, jumping up from his chair. Everyone else jumped too. 'A Klintman! They would never . . .'

'Maybe a Klintman of royal blood, Sire,' said Snori quietly.

There was a silence. The King sat down. His expression changed. He sighed. He said, 'Ralf . . . you mean Ralf.'

'Yes, Sire,' said Snori.

'But surely he wouldn't . . . I mean, he's been very quiet and . . .'

'Planning something like this, Your Majesty, I shouldn't wonder,' said Snori firmly.

The King looked at him. 'You never liked him, did you, my friend?'

'I didn't trust him, Sire.'

The King sighed again. 'And you always wished Gilda might look at you instead of him. I agree, mind you.'

Snori blushed hotly. 'The . . . the Princess Gilda is very kind,' he said quickly. 'She has a good word for everybody.'

'Come on, Snori, say you hate the scoundrel,' said the King, smiling broadly now. 'Look, I have left Ralf alone to spare Gilda's feelings. But if any of you can prove it was Ralf who—'

'No need for any of them to do that,' said a familiar voice, and all at once the door crashed wide open. And there in the doorway, splendidly dressed as ever if a trifle sea-stained, stood the dwarf they'd known as Brock Blackbeard. He was flanked by two enormous, grim-faced trolls, armed with huge swords. And in one hand he gripped the arm of a white-faced Princess Gilda!

SEVENTEEN

King Reidmar sprang up again. 'Ralf Ravenbeard, traitor and son of a traitor, let my daughter go! Your quarrel is not with her!'

'Really, Cousin Reidy,' said Ralf mockingly, 'you should use softer language. Haven't you heard it's not good form – not to speak of unwise – to insult someone who holds all the cards? You should take a leaf out of the book of your Ambassador who now has such a high reputation for charm and fine speaking in Middler lands.'

'Impostor! What have you done with my friend?' hissed the King.

'I don't think I want to tell you just yet,' said

Ralf lightly. 'Now sit down, dear cousin, there's a good chap. Yes, you too,' he said, nodding to the others, who quickly obeyed. Ralf waved the trolls in. They shut and bolted the door and leaned against it. Ralf walked Gilda over to a chair, sat down, and then pulled her on to his knee. 'Sit tight, my beauty,' he said, smiling at her. She glared. He laughed. 'Come on, you like a bold man, my beauty. Now I'll show you just how bold I am . . .'

King Reidmar said in a strangled voice, 'Let my daughter go.'

'I don't intend to until you do certain things for me, old boy. I've waited a long time for this. My, my, what a schemozzle you're in, these days, cousin dear!' he went on. 'I was able to get into your palace easy as winking, everyone seems at sixes and sevens.' He grinned. 'But then maybe you weren't expecting me, were you? Maybe you thought I'd gone gurgle-urgle down to the bottom of the sea along with the boat, eh? You forget – I have good friendships in strange places, cousin dear.'

'I know that well enough,' grated Reidmar. His eyes were icy as green crystal.

Ralf looked at Thomas and the twins. 'Clever little creatures, aren't you?' he said. 'To think you worked it out – or nearly all of it. Suppose you wouldn't want to come and work for me? No? Oh, well, never mind. It'll be one for the scrapbook, eh?' He turned to the Professor. 'As to you, Prof, I can't say I'd tell you to change your day job. Good magician you might be – though personally I'd wonder – but good detective you most certainly are not. How could you think that the *real* Blackbeard could really be involved in anything as daring and clever as this? Old poker-face windbag wouldn't know a good plot if it stood up and hit him in the face.'

He sounds much more slangy, less formal than before, thought Thomas. But he still loves to talk. Gab, gab, gab, yack, yack, yack. Maybe that'll help? Aloud, Thomas said, 'It's all very well to say it was clever but you haven't pulled it off, have you? We found you out, and . . .'

'Oh, my dear little Rymer,' said the dwarf, smiling broadly. 'I said you worked *nearly* all of it out. Not all of it, my friend. You see, your friends in Owlchurch and Aspire are mighty embarrassed right now because they think they didn't spot a slick glamouring job. In fact, the prizes *were* real enough – I simply took them out of the display case and replaced them at the right moment with a few leaves, so it looked like everyone had been taken in by a glamour . . .'

'I thought so!' Pinch burst out. Everyone looked at him. He went red.

'Clever little clogs,' said Ralf lightly. 'But what a pity your friends back home don't know what you worked out, eh? No, I'm afraid they think they were tricked from the beginning. They also know by now that I've disappeared, as has the Professor, and you children. They'll find a "secret" letter I planted for them. And so they'll put two and two together and make five. They'll think that King Reidmar, for reasons of his own, wanted to play a nasty trick against the Middlers, and that the Professor was involved in that, as an agent for him. Me – well, I'll be remembered as the wicked Ambassador, Brock Blackbeard, who rewarded hospitality with lies and trickery. You children – well, you've been kidnapped by King Reidmar's dastardly agents, who are demanding a handsome ransom for you, or else you'll be fed to the sharkfolk of Mirkengrim. Maybe there's even a touch of Uncouther involvement in it all. Nice, eh?'

'You scoundrel. You rogue. You . . . you evil criminal,' panted King Reidmar. His eyes were starting out of his head.

'Dear Cousin Reidy! Such language! I am hurt. But, dear cousin, I'm only giving you in kind the coin you paid my poor father and myself, when you cooked up that plot he was supposedly in with the Uncouthers.'

Snori spoke for the first time. 'There was no

cooking up,' he said softly. 'It was all true beyond a doubt, Ralf Ravenbeard. Have a care, lest you lose even the tiniest shred of honour you have left.'

'Snori Sunbeard, you've always had a small mind,' said Ralf.

Gilda spoke. Her voice was tight. 'Forgive me, Snori. I didn't want to believe you. Now I do.'

'Do you, my beauty?' The black-bearded dwarf's eyes flashed. He gripped Gilda's arm tighter. 'Pity, as you're to be my wife.'

'Never!' said Gilda fiercely, and twisting around suddenly, she hit out sharply at Ralf. He was taken by surprise, and fell back. But before she had time to run, he grabbed her again and motioned to one of the trolls.

'Hold her,' he hissed. Despite Gilda's struggles, the troll dragged her away near the door, while the other one stood with drawn sword, daring anyone to help her.

Ralf took something out of his pocket.

Thomas recognized it at once. It was the Seafolk trader's little amber box. The dwarf opened it and put it on the desk. He took a pinch of the silver seamoon dust and held it up high. He said softly, 'And if anyone tries that kind of trick again, I'll use up this whole box and glamour up the sea into this place. You know that if I do that, the magic conjured up will be so huge that the glamour will become real. It'll sweep everything away – do you hear, Cousin Reidy? Everything!'

'How did you get that?' croaked the King. 'If you got an Uncouther to—'

'Uncouthers, Uncouthers, is that all you can think of? They're not the only ones with grudges, you know, or the only ones with dark talents.' He nodded at the trolls. 'You treat them like fools – but not all of them are. Some I'm proud to call friends.'

'You mean you got a troll to steal it for you? You have fallen even lower than I thought,' spat the King.

'Temper, temper! In my exile, dear cousin, I've learned many things. One's patience. Another is that revenge is a dish best eaten cold. And another is that though for centuries we dwarves have thought trolls are dull and stupid as rocks, we are quite wrong.' He smiled at the troll guards, who beamed rather horribly, showing lots of broken teeth. 'My friends here have been my partners in this enterprise all along. They have cunning as well as strength.'

King Reidmar laughed rather hollowly. 'I have no interest in your theories about trolls,' he snapped. 'Just get this over with. What do you want?'

'My rights,' said Ralf, at once.

'The crown?'

Ralf threw his head back and laughed. 'By Thoran, no! You can keep that poison trap for yourself. I want my father's memory saved from dishonour. I want you to say he was not a traitor and never dealt with Uncouthers. I want to marry your daughter. I want you to give me half of your treasure. Then I will sail away from here with Gilda and my friends and I will never come back. This I promise.'

King Reidmar was grey. There were beads of sweat on his forehead. 'And what will you give me if I agree to these ridiculous demands?'

'Father!' said Gilda, sounding stricken. The King turned his head away. 'What will you give me?' he demanded fiercely.

Thomas was puzzled. Why was the King acting like this? He glanced at the twins, who shrugged slightly, looking as puzzled as he. But Snori and the Professor were frowning, staring first at the King, then at Ralf, who caught their glance.

He said, 'Wonder why he doesn't scream and shout any longer? He's scared, folks. Scared. Scared the truth will come out at last, after all these years.' He strode over to the King, and nobody tried to stop him. 'Here's the deal,' he said. 'I can't give you back the tawdry golden prizes with which you hoped to buy international friendship – they've gone to the bottom of the sea along with your boat. Never mind. I'm sure there's plenty more where they came from! But I will give you back your international standing – I will give you a signed confession.'

Thomas was listening, but also thinking hard. Something had to be done, and soon!

Ralf was still talking. 'And I'll give you back your friend Brock Blackbeard, who's crossly resting, as we speak, where you exiled my father and me – on the island. See, Brock's boat didn't get very far when it set off from here. We hijacked it only a few miles offshore, before he even had a chance to get anywhere near Middler country. We unloaded him and his trolls – they fought hard, I must admit – and left them there, guarded by more of my friends. Then we took their places and sailed off with the prizes to the Convention. What fun it's all been! I reckon I should be the Grand Champion of the Tournament, don't you? My *Hide and Seek* was just about perfect. In fact, I have to admit I enjoyed hoodwinking all you lovely people so much . . .' and here he bowed mockingly to the Professor, Thomas and the twins, 'so much that I'm tempted to throw in an extra offer. I'll guarantee your safe passage back, the four of you. You've given me some good entertainment, and you're brave and – at least you children – clever. Never let it be said Ralf Ravenbeard does not reward these things!'

'You're an arrogant fool,' said Snori quietly. 'That you do get from your father. For Thoran's sake, Ralf, listen! We were once friends. I know your father's betrayal hit you hard. But you must understand, it was true that he—'

'No! It was lies!' shouted Ralf, his face going crimson with fury. 'You have been tricked by the real traitor – him!' He pointed dramatically at King Reidmar. 'He plotted to get the throne from Father. He set him up with false deals with Uncouthers. I've had it straight from them, from Grimgrod and the others!'

'Straight?' snorted the Professor, speaking at last. 'Grimgrod can't lie straight in bed, or any of his friends! Lies and deceit are their pleasures. They know the truth about Magnus, that he was their ally. They just love to stir up trouble.'

'Good,' said Ralf, smiling. 'They'll *get* trouble. The Middlers will be furious with them. They'll suspect Uncouthers were in on this too. They'll be banned from the Conventions now for ever.'

'You fool,' said the Professor, shaking his head sadly. 'You've acted more shamefully than any Uncouther. Do you want the whole of the Hidden World against you?'

'I don't care,' snapped Ralf. 'Anyway, what do you know, old man? You've been outwitted and upstaged by a bunch of children!'

'I know that,' said the Professor humbly, 'and I hope they'll forgive me for being a stubborn old bossy boots about it all . . .'

'Very touching. But enough of this,' said Ralf impatiently. 'Cousin dear, I'm waiting. Do we have a deal?'

There was a silence. Everyone looked at King Reidmar, who stood with his head bent, looking somehow older and shrunken. Ralf Ravenbeard was smiling, sure of himself.

'Snori told me you hated me. I didn't really believe it,' said the King at last, in a small voice.

'Fool! Of course I hate you! More – I despise you. You took the throne by deceit. Now you are exposed as the worm you truly are.'

'Oh, Ralf,' said the King wearily, 'hate must be a terrible burden.'

'I wear it lightly,' said Ralf.

Thomas felt uneasy. Why wasn't the King just refusing? Was he playing for time? Or could it be – could it be that Ralf was right? He looked over at Gilda, whose face was white and set, her eyes blank and expressionless. He looked at Pinch and Patch, whose faces wore a look of utter dismay, and at the Professor and Snori, who looked anxious. Only Ralf and the trolls – who were grinning broadly, obviously enjoying this – looked relaxed.

'Don't think anyone's coming to save you,' said Ralf, into the silence. 'I've woven a good strong spell-net around this room. None of your guards can reach us. Nor any of your people. And there's no one coming from abroad to save you . . .'

Suddenly, Thomas's mind cleared. He'd had a marvellous idea! Would it work? He put a stealthy hand into his pocket. Yes, the sliver of glass was still there – and the leaf. He eyed the amber box on the desk. He had to signal to the twins. But they were staring at Ralf and the King.

Reidmar spoke. 'Oh, Ralf, I wish you hadn't . . .'

'Hadn't exposed you? Of course you wish I hadn't! But I have! Now stop stalling and tell me – what is your answer?'

At that moment, Patch turned her head. She caught Thomas's glance. She saw him nod, very slightly, towards the amber box on the desk, then cautiously pat his pocket. Thomas mouthed, 'Glass – ice . . .' Her eyes widened.

She gave a tiny nod. She nudged Pinch.

Nobody else saw any of this – all their attention was fixed on the two opponents. Ralf was smiling, sure of victory now. But the King was looking more weary and beaten than ever. At last he said, 'I am so sorry, everyone, but I am going to have to—'

At that moment, Pinch sprang. In an instant, he had the box open. Thomas pulled out the glass from his pocket and threw it on the floor, at Ralf's feet. Patch yelled something, very high. Pinch threw wild pinches of seamoon dust in the air. Instantly, the sliver of glass became a huge slippery sheet of ice that shot across the room. Ralf, the trolls and Gilda fell over in a heap. The trolls' swords went skidding across the ice and landed at the twins' feet. They shoved them under the desk.

The trolls and Ralf kept slipping and sliding, trying to get up. But Gilda slid swiftly on her bottom away to the edge of the ice. Meanwhile, the King, the Professor and Snori made a lunge at Ralf, who rolled over and over, away from them. Slithering on their bellies, the trolls tried to help him. It looked like they might succeed. Thomas shouted, 'Pinch! Patch! The leaf! A blanket!'

Pinch grabbed more seamoon dust and flung it as Thomas threw the leaf up. Instantly, it became a choking brown blanket, falling on top of all the people struggling on the ice. It was sheer chaos!

Just then, there was an almighty crack. Under the pressure of the ice, the door had splintered! The sheet of ice shook, shimmered, and vanished with a huge pop. Not even the sliver of glass remained. The blanket disappeared in a twinkling, leaving only shredded bits of leaf. But Ralf and the trolls had no time to escape, for a crowd of Klintmen came bursting in, who soon made short work of catching and tying them up.

'Sire, what shall we do with these traitors?' said Snori.

The King had his arm around his daughter.

He turned his head away from the captives. He said wearily, 'Take them to the dungeons.'

Ralf was bruised and white, his hair and beard awry. But he still managed to draw himself up and say, 'I will die proudly, without the shame you bear on your soul.'

Snori took a step towards him, eyes flashing. The King waved a hand to stop him. 'Why do you speak of dying?' he said quietly, his eyes meeting Ralf's.

'You will put me and my friends to death, of course,' spat Ralf. 'But know we are not afraid and —'

'Oh, shut up,' said the King, without heat. 'You talk too much, Ralf. Even for one of our people, you talk too much. You always did. And you act like a silly boy, not a grown man. Now go and cool your heels in prison. You'll have time enough to think then.'

For the first time, Ralf looked uncertain. 'I will tell you nothing,' he began. 'I won't sign a confession or—'

'You don't need to. You've already told us everything,' broke in the King. 'You couldn't resist it, could you, gabbing about how clever you were? You've told us how you did it, where you're holding Brock, what happened to the prizes, everything, my poor deluded Ralf.' He looked taller, somehow, thought Thomas, amazed. The strength and power he'd seen there, at first, had come back. The King looked every inch a King.

'You . . . you . . .' spluttered Ralf, going red. 'You tricked me . . . you . . .' He tried to master himself. 'But it doesn't matter. The damage has been done. The Middlers – or anyone else – will never trust you again. Your name will be mud in all the Hidden World.'

'Rubbish!' said the Professor fiercely. 'The children and I are witnesses to everything too, don't forget. It won't be the King's name that's mud, but yours.'

'In any case,' said the King, 'I will tell the Middlers the truth, and we'll see.'

Ralf laughed bitterly. 'The truth! What do you know of truth?'

'Poor Ralf,' said the King quietly. 'You have done a bad thing. But I'm afraid I did do wrong by you in the past. You were not involved in your father's wicked schemes. I should not have exiled you.'

Ralf's mouth opened. He tried to speak, but no words came out. Thomas suddenly saw tears spring into his eyes. He met the dwarf's glance for a moment. Then Ralf Ravenbeard turned his head away, and said coldly, 'Well, what are you waiting for? Take me and my friends away. I am tired of the company here.'

Without another word, the King signalled to the guards. Everyone watched in silence as Ralf and the trolls were marched away, Ralf still with his head held high, but the trolls with their heads bent, shuffling along very reluctantly indeed.

EIGHTEEN

After a little while, Thomas asked, 'What are you going to do with him, Your Majesty?'

'Put him on trial, I suppose,' said the King, sighing. 'I wish . . . oh dear . . .' His eyes met Snori's. 'You must understand – you were once Ralf's friend, and I saw him grow up. He was a good enough lad then. He had many talents. I am very sorry that his father's crimes so embittered his life. He did not deserve it. He had done nothing. I should not have exiled him. I should not have listened to Brock. He was very definite it must happen.'

'That's as maybe,' said Snori, 'but Ralf did not have to take the path he took.'

'No, no, I know that. Well! He'll have to be put on trial, and punished – I suggest he should be put to work in the mines for a spell – but then we'll have to free him. We'll have to give him a second chance.' He turned to his silent daughter. 'What do you think, Gilda?'

'It's up to you, Father,' she said rather coldly. 'I have no feeling for Ralf Ravenbeard any more.'

'No, no,' said the King, patting her hand and smiling broadly. 'I quite understand. I thought maybe you and Snori . . .'

Gilda glared at her father, as Snori went bright red. 'Don't matchmake!' she snapped.

'Not at all, my dear. I was about to say you and Snori can accompany me on our voyage to the land of the Middlers, that's all,' said her father, with a little twinkle in his eye. 'I think we should start there as soon as possible – but not before we've collected together some more prizes to take with us, don't you think so, my friends?' he added, smiling.

'Oh, yes! I think that would be an excellent idea!' burst out Pinch.

'Wonderful!' said Patch.

'Oh – and of course you children must have a reward,' said the King cheerfully. 'Your glamouring spell was so strong it quite overcame the much more minor spell Ralf put on the palace. We owe our safety to you. Ask for anything you like.'

Thomas and Pinch and Patch looked at each other. But it was Thomas who said slowly, 'Your Majesty, I think there's something we'd all like to do – and the Professor too,' he added. 'And that's to see something no non-Klint has ever seen: the original treasures of the Klint-Kingdom, and the dragon who guards them.'

'Oh, yes,' breathed Pinch and Patch, eyes shining. The Professor said nothing, but his eyes were like stars.

The King looked hard at Thomas. Then he looked at the painting above his desk. There was a little silence. The King's face slowly relaxed into a smile. 'Well, well, what a lovely idea,' he said brightly. 'A most fitting reward! I am more than happy to grant it! Now – no time like the present! Let's go there right away!'

The steps went down, down, down in the darkness. The light from the blazebird lamps that they carried was only just enough for them to see their way down. The air began to grow thicker and heavier, and a strange hot smell began to waft around them. Thomas started to feel a little scared. The smell reminded him of being in the Uncouthers' dark city, Pandemonium. He tried to keep a grip on himself. This was quite different . . . He was safe here. Safe.

Down the steps wound, and down. Then just as Thomas thought they could not go down any further, the stairs ended. They had come to a small, hot room, with a thick, opaque black glass floor and rocky walls. On one side of the room was what looked like an elevator shaft.

The King beckoned them all forward. 'It's not safe for non-Klints to go any further down,' he said, 'but if you look down through the observation floor, you will see everything.' He touched the black glass, and at once it slid back, revealing another thick layer of glass underneath, but clear as crystal this time. Thomas and the twins pressed forward, the Professor close behind them.

They looked down into what seemed to be a deep, rocky cave. It glistened like a living jewel, with stalactites and stalagmites that shone not just white but all kinds of flashing colours. In the middle of the cave was a great raised box, with a crystal bottom and a golden top. Sprawled across the top of it, with its eyes closed, was a large, magnificent dragon with scales like living red-gold and whose elegant wings were like embroidered cloth of gold.

At first, Thomas could see nothing but the beauty and majesty of the dragon. Then, as his eyes adjusted to the light, he saw that the

crystal box held something. Closer, and he saw them at last: the sword of Sindrini, the dagger of Daini and the necklace of Nissa. They were many, many times bigger than the replicas he'd seen in the Institute of Illusion. And if those had been the most beautiful things he'd seen then, he knew now that their beauty was nothing compared to the originals. It was as if someone had taken rays of sunlight and all the ancient fires of the earth, and poured them into these graceful, powerful shapes.

'Good gracious me,' said the Professor wonderingly. 'Did you ever see anything like that?'

Just then, the dragon opened one eye, then another. The iris was red as fire, the pupil bright gold. The dragon looked straight up at Thomas and the twins. They could feel the sudden heat of those eyes, as if an oven had just opened. Pinch and Patch took a step back, followed very quickly by the Professor.

'Isn't it amazing . . . ?' breathed Patch.

'Isn't it just?' quavered Pinch.

'Just a bit hot, though . . .' faltered the Professor, turning back hastily to the other adults.

But Thomas looked straight into the dragon's eyes one instant more. All at once, he heard a voice in his mind. A growling, hot sort of voice, that he felt sure was the voice of the dragon. 'Good day to you, Rymer, friend of the Klint-Kingdom,' said the voice. 'Never forget this. Everyone has a treasure to find. You too. And when you find it, guard it well.'

It looked at Thomas one instant longer. Then one eye closed, and another, and the dragon fell asleep once more.

'Thomas?' said Patch a little anxiously. 'Are you all right?'

'Oh, I'm just fine,' said Thomas, as he took one last look at the three treasures. 'I was just thinking, that's all. Thinking how glad I'll be when we're home.'

'You can say that again!' said Pinch heartily.